Destiny's Journey Fate or Faith

RB Parkline

Published by RB Parkline, 2024.

DESTINY'S JOURNEY FATE OR FAITH

First edition. October 31, 2024.

Copyright © 2024 RB Parkline.

ISBN: 979-8227638939

Written by RB Parkline.

Chapter I

Traven sat in the dimly lit pub staring at the wooden cup half filled with rum. He sighed heavily as he looked around. Men were laughing and talking loudly. Some were gambling others sat quietly getting drunker as the night wore on. They had all come out of a war that was hell. The battles were always up close and personal. Swords and daggers slashing and stabbing. Death of the enemy was the only goal. Battlefields were littered with dead bodies. Men hacked to death, many of them with mortal wounds lay dying with blood thick on the ground. Men screaming in agony, crying for their mothers, or wifes, some praying, others lay quietly waiting for death to take them. Then it ended, and the soldiers were sent home. What were soldiers to do now they were no longer needed. They had no purpose.

The smell of ham and potatoes lingered in the air which was the dinner special. The aroma of rum and body odor mingled with the diner special hung heavy in the air. He was bored. It was the same each night.

He saw Beth pick up wooden tankards from a table that men had been sitting at earlier. She looked up smiling at him. Her dark hair framed her small pretty face. Her low cut dress showed her bosom, and curves. She was the only thing in the small village that mattered to him. Beth worked at the pub that was an inn with beds upstairs, and also served food.

Beth walked over to Travens table with a pitcher. Traven smiled slightly, waving his hand. Beth looked at the wooden cup half full and smiled. She walked toward another table with men laughing, filling larger tankards with rum. Her father owned the inn which she and her sister both worked. Her sister Darla who was older worked in the back cooking. Darla and her husband would inherit the inn when her father passed away.

The big heavy front door opened as a woman walked inside the inn. She was dressed in black leather pants and a cotton shirt. She had a long cloak with a hood covering her head. A sword moved freely as she walked. The dust on her clothes indicated she was riding a horse. Most women traveled in carriages or wagons.

A large man followed the woman. He was six foot six and over two hundred fifty pounds. He had black leather pants and a black leather shirt. His cloak had an insignia of a battle ax and a mace. The broad sword he wore was massive. He followed the woman to a table and sat across from her.

The woman removed the hood covering her head. Every man stared at the beautiful woman, as she removed her cloak, hanging it on the back of her chair. The large man sat down removing his cloak allowing it to lay on the floor.

Traven froze in place. Time seemed to stand still as he stared at the man. He was wearing the insinga of the Royal Rangers. Travens mind raced, it was impossible the Royal Rangers had all been killed. The Rangers were the most elite fighting force in the Wixon army. The last of them had been killed in the battle of the lower meadows. Five hundred had stood against six thousand. When it was over only twenty two hundred of the enemy had survived. The war had ended shortly after that battle.

Traven knew the Royal Rangers were trained at a young age. If the man was not six foot four they were not accepted as a Ranger. Their training was said to have been intense. He could not believe he was seeing a Ranger in the small inn.

Beth walked to the table and smiled nervously. The woman looked at her intently. With dark eyes. Beth said "the special is ham and shredded potatoes." The woman nodded and looked away. Beth looked at the big man who only stared at her. The woman did not look at Beth, she said in a soft voice. "I require a room with clean sheets."

"I wash the sheets daily, my lady." Beth said, obviously offended.

The woman turned and looked at her without speaking. "One room and wine with the diner."

Beth looked at the big man who only stared back at her. "Water with his meal." the woman said in a firm quiet voice.

A young man walked up to the table as Beth walked away. He pulled up a chair sitting down. Tomlin, was a local thug, who had a high opinion of himself. He had fought in the war as it was ending. He let all know how he had been in many battles and had killed many men. He was a braggart Traven had recently warned him to stop bothering Beth. Tomlin grinned and walked away in his cocky manner. He listened to Traven and stopped talking to Beth.

Traven set up as he watched Tomlin. The big man leaned forward, bringing up his hand back, handing Tomlin across the face. The blow knocked Tomlin out of his chair, sending him crashing hard on the floor. Tomlin scrambled to his feet, his hand on his dagger. Blood running from his nose he stared at the big man with rage in his eye. The man did not move as he looked back at Tomlin with contempt in his dark eyes.

The woman turned her head and said in her soft voice. "You were not invited." She had an accent that Traven recognized. He thought it strange she and the Ranger were there.

She turned and looked away. Tomlin stood staring at the back of the woman's head then to the man. He turned looking at Traven who watched him. Tomlin walked away sitting at a table with other men. He wiped blood from his nose and yelled for more rum.

BETH RETURNED TO THE table with a platter. She sat a plate in front of the lady and the man. A small goblet which was half full of wine in front of the lady and a cup of water in front of the man. She watched the man with a spoon dip it in the woman's potatoes and move it to his mouth. Beth walked away.

Later Beth walked to the table picking up the empty plates. She asked if the woman would like more wine. The woman pushed the goblet toward her. The woman asked. "Do you know of a guide that can escort us across the mountains?"

Beth looked at the beautiful woman with dark complexion and dark wavy hair.

"The mountains are dangerous, my lady. There is a pass." Beth hesitated as she looked into the dark eyes. "I know of only one man." Beth looked over her shoulder at Traven.

"I would like to speak to him." the lady said as she looked at Traven.

Beth carried the platter to the back then returned, going to Traven. She placed her hand on his shoulder leaning down saying "The lady would like to speak to you concerning the pass across the mountains."

Traven was surprised. He looked at Beth who said softly. "Be careful."

Traven stood up and walked to the table. He stopped and asked "May I approach my lady?"

She nodded.

Traven walked to the table, picked up the chair that was turned over and sat down. He looked at the big man realizing he was the biggest man he had ever seen. He could not help but look at the insignia. He turned to look at the woman who was looking directly at him. He looked at her ears seeing both had a slight point. It was what he had expected, the dark skin, dark eyes, her accent he thought to himself she was Wixon. They were a race of people who it was said practiced magic. They had fought with his king. Many had been killed in the war. They lived across the sea on a large island. He noticed she was lighter than most of the Wixon he had met.

"I am in need of a guide to take me and my companion across the mountains." She said, speaking low, studying Traven.

"It's a dangerous journey. There are two passes. The northern pass is the shortest route if you are going to Sistera. The southern pass will be closer to Kachita. It is late in the season and the possibilities of them being closed by snow is a real chance. Should it snow later in the year the passes will be clear. Then there are the bandits and thugs that will attempt to rob you. Mountain lions, bears and other predators. Mice will be drawn to the food you carry. Which will attract snakes, all of them are poisonous. The trails are narrow. Horses, mules and men fall off into deep ravines. Cold at night, little water. It is not a walk in a meadow. It will take two cycles of the full moon to cross. Going around the mountain will take you nine months. It is not a pleasant journey but it is safer."

"How do you know the passes?" The big man asked in a low forceful growling voice.

Traven turned and looked directly at the man's face. It was tanned with bushy eyebrows and a full neatly kept beard. The eyes were dark and scars across the face. His nose appeared to have been broken several times.

"My father Evan Tisdale was a merchant. He made the trip many times when I was younger. His last trip was when I was fourteen. When he arrived in Kachita the new regent demanded my father accept a price that was much less than what was desirable. My father politely refused. He was murdered in his sleep that night. I was taken to the coast and placed on a ship where I worked for many years. I left and joined the army under Chamberlain."

The big man stared at Traven without blinking. He looked at the woman and nodded slightly. The woman smiled. "I will pay you twenty pieces of silver if you guide us to Kachita."

Traven was stunned. He would have accepted eight pieces of silver. "I will need you to make all the arrangements. When can we leave?"

"Day after tomorrow. Fifteen good men would be enough for the trip." Traven looked around the inn that was quiet. All the men were watching him. He looked back at the big Ranger. "I would recommend we take thirty. Most will leave after two weeks. Others will die fighting bandits or will fall off the mountain. Those that do make it to Kachita you can pay off. You should pay them their full amount when we arrive, not before as most will want half their pay before we leave."

"Agreed." The woman said as she stood up. The big man stood up as well.

Beth walked to the two strangers as they followed her up the stairs. Beth stopped at a door opening it. She stepped back as the woman walked inside. She turned looking over her shoulder saying "thank you."

The big man shut the door and stood outside the door with his back to the door. Beth walked away.

Later that evening Traven drained the rum in the small cup and walked upstairs. He saw the big Ranger sitting on the hard floor with his head down leaning against a door. He walked past the Ranger to the room at the end of the hallway. He stepped inside and undressed crawling into bed. He lay quiet in the bed thinking of the journey across the mountains. It would be difficult. He heard the door open and watched as Beth walked in and undressed. She crawled into bed next to Traven. She moved close to him, her arm around his chest.

"Was that a Ranger?" She whispered.

Traven pulled her closer. "Yes I believe it was."

"I thought they were all killed in the battle of the lower meadow." she whispered.

"I did too, but evidently one has survived."

"The woman is beautiful." Beth said as she held Traven.

"I believe she is Wixon." Traven said quietly in the dark.

"Why would a Wixon be this far Northeast, and travel with a Ranger?"

Traven kissed her. "I don't know."

Chapter II

Traven woke up early. He was alone Beth had left earlier. He stepped out of bed dressing in the dim light. He walked out of his room seeing the big Ranger leaning against the door with his head down. Traven walked quietly past the big man. He was amazed to see the Ranger. He was obviously protecting the lady. It seemed strange to him the lady who was obviously Wixon, or at least half Wixon in the village of Solace, at the foot of the large mountains. He wondered why she wanted to go to Kachita. It didn't matter to him. He would make more money in two cycles of the moon than he could in five years, if he survived. He stopped at the end of the hallway knowing he would have to tell Beth. He knew it would devastate her.

Beth brought him breakfast and smiled at him. When he finished she sat down as he explained he would be going across the mountains escorting the big Ranger and the lady. Beth frowned and tried to convince him not to go. She had tears in her eyes as she looked off. "You're leaving, I'll stay and wait for you to return, but you won't. Darla will inherit the inn with her husband. I'll work for them as a servant. Perhaps I will share my bed with another man until he leaves me. The tears streamed down her cheeks. Traven told her he would make enough money they could go anywhere they wanted and start over. Beth looked back at Traven. "It's too dangerous. Please don't go."

Traven stood up walking to her and kissed her on the cheek. "I'll be okay."

He walked out of the Inn.

Traven walked to the outskirts of town to the large house of Brian Heady. He saw the older man outside talking to several men. Brian frowned seeing Traven.

"You're late."

"I know, I just came to tell you I'll be leaving."

"You can't leave, I need you. There are thieves who are stealing my sheep and cattle. I need you to protect them."

"Find someone else. I'm leaving. Just wanted you to know." Traven walked off as Brian followed him begging him to stay.

Traven talked to several merchants buying supplies for the trip. He talked to men he chose to hire, Including Tomlin, concerning the journey across the mountains. He warned them it would be dangerous. The pay would be six pieces of silver when they arrived. All of the men accepted his offer. He was able to find twenty four. He knew all of them had fought in the war. Only a few had actually been on the front lines. Shawn Souls, and Paul Dorman he knew had seen battle. Tomlin was a braggart, but he had fought in the war.

With all of the men gathered late in the morning Traven looked at all of them. They were a rough looking bunch. He took a deep breath allowing it to escape slowly.

"Men this is going to be a rough journey. You need to be prepared for cold nights, bandits that will attack us and wild animals. You are being paid and paid well to escort a lady across the mountains. I would suggest you not talk to her. She is beautiful and yes all of us desire her. None of us would stand a chance with her. We are ruffians who she will have nothing to do with. Keep in mind the big man she travels with is no doubt a Ranger. He will kill you in a moment if you are out of line with her. I don't know her name, or why she wants to go to Kachita. She pays well, that's all that matters. Do your job, stay alive and we get paid. Mind your manners or the big Ranger will kill you. It's up to you." Traven looked at Tomlin and smiled. He told the men to meet him tomorrow morning in front of the Inn and to bring their horse packed for a journey.

Traven walked to the blacksmith's shop that was also a livery stable looking at the horses and mules. He told the blacksmith Bill Doughan he would purchase six mules and three donkeys. Bill was a hard man and drove a hard bargain. Traven shook his head, refusing to pay the high price. He didn't really care what the price was knowing the Lady would pay whatever was needed. He knew Bill was a greedy man and Traven did not want to be cheated .

Traven shook his head disgustedly saying, "no, Bill I'll talk to some of the farmers and buy their stock. You are wanting too much for these scraggly animals."

Bill's face was red with rage. He argued asTraven walked off. Then he backed down, reluctantly accepting Traven's price.

Bill turned and yelled for Micha. A small boy ran to him which Bill slapped hard. Micha fell to the ground. "Where have you been, boy. I need you to gather the mules and donkeys and put them in the big corral. Now move, before I give you a beating!"

Micha stood up rubbing his cheek. He quickly ran to the pens and began moving the animals to the big corral.

Traven found the lady and Ranger sitting outside the inn on the large porch. He told her of the arrangements he had made. She gave him several pieces of silver to pay for the supplies.

With the silver in his purse, Traven paid all the merchants. He told Micha if he would load all the mules and donkeys with the supplies that had been delivered to the corrals. He would give him a silver coin. Micha looked up at the tall man and asked. "Could I come with you Traven? I'm a good groomsman, and I can take care of all the animals."

Traven shook his head. "No, I'm sorry Micha this is a dangerous journey. It would be best to stay with your father."

"He's not my father. I'm an orphan. I work for Bill for a bed and little food. He's meaner than a snake. I want to go. You will need a good groomsman. I promise I will not be any trouble." Micha pleaded.

"Micha, there you are!" Bill walked up and grabbed the small boy throwing him to the ground. The stalls need to be cleaned, you little worthless turd!"

Traven grabbed Bill by the shirt and threw him to the ground. Bill looked at him shocked as he stood up angrily. "Now you know how Micha feels." Traven pushed Bill away from him. He looked at Micha "we will leave early tomorrow, have the supplies packed. You need to pack light, six pieces of silver are yours when we arrive at Kachita, if you survive."

Micha grinned as Traven walked away.

Chapter III

The lady walked down the stairs into the main room wearing leather pants and a cotton shirt. Her long black clock tied around her shoulders. Walking to the older man with gray hair sitting at a table she placed a silver coin on the table and walked away. The older man stared in disbelief at the coin. He had expected five copper coins. The lady walked to where Beth was picking up empty bowls. She placed a silver coin in her small hand. Beth looked surprised.

"Thank you for the clean sheets, and for washing my clothes. She could see the tears in Beth's eyes. "Where's your faith? Do you not pray to the Lord?"

"I do and will continue to pray for Traven." Beth said, speaking just above a whisper.

"Will you also remember me in your prayers?" The lady asked with a slight smile.

"Of course I will pray for you, my lady."

She smiled "thank you." She touched her face with her small hand, closed her eyes and began to chant. "I give you a blessing and will pray for you." She said as she turned and walked away.

The big Ranger had stepped outside seeing the men assembled. He did not smile as he looked at the men. He mumbled to himself "riff-raff."

The lady walked out of the inn and down the steps to her horse that was saddled. She raised her leg as the Ranger grasped the leg lifting her onto her horse. She pulled the hood over her head.

Tomlin with a sneer said "I don't suppose it would be too much to ask my lady's name. We are all going to die on this journey. Can we at least know who it is we give our lives for?"

"Six pieces of silver is all you need to know Tomlin." Traven said as he stepped into the stirrup swinging into the saddle. "Perhaps you would like the Rangers name. Maybe he will tuck you in at night. Tell you a story."

Tomlin's face turned red as he glared at Traven. "Well, let's be on our way then." The big Ranger and the lady beside Traven moved forward. She looked at Micha sitting on a mule. He was holding a rope attached to the mules along with the donkeys

"Micha's the groomsman. He saddled your horse." Traven looked at the big Ranger. "Do you know any bedtime stories, big man?"

"Only horror stories." He said gruffly.

THEY TRAVELED ON THE flat plains for half a day then began the gradual climb up the mountain. It was late in the afternoon and stayed hot until the sun began to go down. Traven did not stop until it was late in the evening. He stopped at a small lake saying they would stop for the night.

Micha unpacked the animals and began to rub them down. He watched as the beautiful woman walked to the lake washing her face, neck and arms. He made sure the animals were tied with a leather strap with a steak driven into the ground close to the water. When they were fed he started a fire and began to cook a meal.

Micha carrying a plate of food walked to the lady handing it to her. She smiled accepting the food.

"Bring me a plate boy." Tomlin snapped.

Micha pointed to the fire. "You can get your own."

Traven walked to the food and began filling his plate. "It looks good, Micha. I expected the men to cook for themselves. We should be thankful you can cook. The Big Ranger stared at Tomlin and the men. Each of them walked to the fire and filled their own plate.

It grew dark as the men laid out their blankets close to the fire. Micha took his blanket to the mules and donkeys sleeping close to them. Tomlin stared at the lady as she lay down. One of the men said "I bet she could keep a man warm."

Tomlin sneered at him. "Sleep with that witch and your manhood would fall off."

"That's no big thing is it Tomlin. I mean really just a small thing."

Tomlin snapped his head around seeing it was Traven who spoke. He glared at Traven who stared back at him. The other men laughed as they lay under their blankets.

The days were warm, traveling was slow as the caravan of men with the lady made their way up the mountain. The evenings became cooler as the sun set. It was a peaceful trip and there was no sign of problems. The first week and a half was uneventful.

By the second week the lush grass began to fade as the trees were no longer seen. The group had to lean forward in their saddles as the trail became steeper. Traven began to feel uneasy as the days passed as they moved higher in the mountains.

In the third week late in the night the sound of a donkey braying loudly woke the men from their sleep. The mules and donkeys were braying as a mountain lion had come into the camp. Micha seeing the mountain lion with his sling twirling it quickly above his head released the rock striking the large cat on his neck. Angry at being seen and the small boy striking him with a rock infuriated the large beast. He charged. The lion was close when it fell and staggered to get up. Paul Dorman, who was on watch, shot the lion with an arrow. He shot again as the animal screamed in pain. Traven ran up to the animal and killed it with his sword. He saw Micha was tending to the animals, attempting to settle them down. He walked to Micha, "You alright Micha?"

"Yes, I'm okay, thanks to Paul."

"I'm sorry Micha, I should have had more men on duty to help protect the animals." he looked at Paul. "Thank you Paul."

Paul nodded and walked off.

The men made their way back to their blankets except for Shawn who would stand guard with Paul.

The following morning the men ate a light breakfast. Traven warned the men to be prepared for not only wild animals but bandits who were no doubt aware of them. MIcha felt a hand on his head. He looked up seeing the large man looking down at him. The big Ranger patted him on the head and walked off.

As they rode the lady moved her horse next to Micha.

"You were brave last night Micha."

His face turned red as he looked down. "Thank you, my lady. I was trying to protect the animals and thought I could scare off the Lion. I'm glad Paul is a good archer."

She smiled "you were brave, most men would have ran to protect themselves." She watched the small boy. "Why are you here Micha?"

"I'm an orphan and thought I could make some money and I don't know maybe start a life in Katchita."

She smiled. "What will you do?"

"I'm not sure," he said, lowering his voice. "I'll ask Traven."

That evening as they stopped there was no water or grass. Traven told the group they would need to conserve their water since the next water was two days.

The following morning as the group prepared to leave Traven told Paul to choose ten men and follow the trail that went west. They would not take their horses. He would continue to head North with the main group. He told Paul that he would need to move north along the rocks keeping out of sight looking for bandits. Traven said he was concerned since there was a small opening ahead of them. It would be a good place for an ambush. Traven frowned saying "When you hear a battle you and your men will need to attack from the rear. Take good archers with you."

The trail became narrow so the group had to ride single file. Traven watched the rocks knowing they were close to the narrow opening. He told the men to be careful and keep a lookout for bandits. The big Ranger moved closer to the lady. He told Micha to stay close to him.

Late in the afternoon a man yelled "men on the rocks!" Traven was off his horse and running up the hill with his sword in his hand. Other men were following him as arrows began to rain down. Horses and mules began to buck as men came out from behind the rocks. They were met by Traven and the men following him. The big Ranger with his broad sword swinging soon had the bandits running. They were met by Paul and his men. The battle was fierce as men fell. Soon the bandits were fleeing for their lives. Micha stayed behind and held the animals. The lady was off her horse helping Micha with the horses.

The men returned with six men hurt. Traven instructed the men to mount up and ride. He knew there were no doubt more bandits. They rode throughout the day and into the night. They finally stopped by a small stream.

The wounded were cared for as the exhausted group lay down. The lady with Micha helping wrapped the wounded men with rags. She explained as she placed a powder on the wound how it would help the wounds heal.

"Is it magic?" Micha asked.

The lady smiled. "No, there is no such thing as Magic. These are healing herbs."

Early the next morning Traven and most of the men went out looking for the bandits. They found the men sitting around a campfire. They attacked, surprising the men and although outnumbered the bandits were defeated. The fighting was hard fought as the bandits fought back fiercely. Those who survived escaped running for their lives. Traven and the Ranger followed them and the ones they found, died.

They returned to camp where Traven told the group they would take a break and rest the animals, starting early in the morning. Four of the men were killed in the battle with the bandits. The following morning five men had left in the middle of the night. The rest of the group continued on their journey.

Chapter IV

The group was up early. No one spoke as the day wore on as it had turned colder. The men were all in a somber mood, all of them lost in their own thoughts. They were surprised when Traven stopped at a creek in the early afternoon. The grass and flowers close to the clear swift stream was a beautiful sight.

When the fires were started Traven explained there was a steep incline not far. They would rest and prepare for the dangerous climb in the morning. No one spoke as they rested near the stream.

Micha had prepared a stew and as usual he dipped a large portion in a bowl taking it to the lady. As he approached he suddenly stopped. He slowly sat the bowl on the ground as the others watched. He reached for his small knife in a sheath he wore on his side. With a quick motion threw the knife toward the lady.

A large black snake rose quickly out of the grass flopping on the ground. The small knife had struck it behind its head. The lady moved quickly away from it. Shawn walked to the snake as did the Ranger and Traven. Shawn stepped on the snake's head and cut it off with a smooth stroke with his large dagger. He picked up the snake's body removing the small knife. Shawn carried it to Micha handing him his knife. He handed the large black snake's body to Micha saying, "you killed it, you can skin it."

Micha dropped the snake picking up the bowl, taking it to the lady who stood behind the Ranger. She accepted the bowl with a shaking hand. Micha walked back picking up the snake and began to remove the skin.

Micha looked up seeing the big Ranger standing over him. He looked up at the giant of a man who reached out with a large dagger saying, "You need a knife that will kill, not one that wounds." Micha stared at the dagger in a leather sheath. "Go ahead, take it," the Ranger said.

Micha stood up taking the dagger. He untied the thin leather strap pulling the dagger out. The blade was close to eight inches, shining and razor sharp. The handle was smooth wood with a silver hilt. It was a beautiful knife. He replaced it in the sheath and looked at the big Ranger who smiled at him.

The lady walked up taking the dagger and placed it around his waist tying it securely. She said softly, "it is a Ranger's dagger. All Rangers are required to make their own dagger." She placed her hand on his face and smiled. Bowing her head she began to chant softly. When she finished she looked at him. "A blessing for you my friend. Thank you." She kissed him on the cheek.

SHAWN SAT HIS BOWL down saying, "I cut the snake's head off, my lady."

She walked to Shawn and going to her knees placed her hand on the rough sun baked face and bowing began to chant. When she finished she kissed him on the cheek. "Thank you Shawn."

Traven said "You know I did help start the fire for dinner."

She stood up walking away looking at him saying "I pray for you each evening. You need it."

Micha cut large chunks of white meat from the black snake. He gathered long slender sticks which he placed the thick meat on the ends and pushed them in the ground. He leaned the white meat close to the fire. He turned them occasionally, allowing the meat to cook evenly. When it was brown he picked up a stick and walked to the lady handing her the stick with the brown snake meat on the end. She accepted it and stared at it as Micha walked away. The Ranger leaned over taking the stick.

"It's really quite good."

The other men each went and also took a stick sitting near the fire and began to eat the cooked snake meat.

The men sitting around the fire talked in low tones.

Tomlin smiled saying "When we get to Katchita, I'm going to a brothel and spend a week there giving those girls a treat." Paul laughed. Tomlin glared at him. "What's so funny?"

"You really think you're gonna make it out of this journey alive?" Paul said, dropping his smile.

"Yeah I do." Tomollin said defensively. "If you survive, what will you do with your silver?"

"Get drunk," Paul said looking down.

Aaron Baker said "I'm buying a boat. Heading for the deep blue sea and fish." He looked at Daren, his twin, "you can be my first mate."

"Okay we will go in cahoots." Daren said grinning.

The conversation of the men soon became quiet. Tomlin, looking at the lady, asked as he leaned back. "So my lady, why won't you tell us your name?"

She looked at him with no emotion. "There is a reason why I won't tell you."

"What's the reason," he asked?

"I don't want to." She said not smiling.

"You're Wixon. your people practice magic." Tomlin said, sneering.

She smiled then laughed. "You are a superstitious fool. There is no such thing as magic. My people practice holistic medicine. We use the plants God has given the world to heal. Our prayers are chants in our native language. Only weak minded fools who are too ignorant to understand believe in witches."

Tomlins face was red with rage.

"Careful how you respond my foolish friend."

He snapped his head around seeing Traven looking directly at him. "Wixon people are not only healers, they are warriors. She can no doubt kill you with little effort."

No one spoke as the tension in the air was now thick.

"She was at the lower meadows with her people when Rangers were defeated. My lady brought me back to life after they had tracked down King Axel's army and destroyed them." The Ranger said quietly.

"You were not dead, Rubean. You were close to death, but I was able to heal your wounds by the grace of God. You should not say such things as being brought back to life. No one can be brought back from death. The ignorant will believe you were resurrected from the dead."

"You know I did hear a story one time of a man who was brought back from the dead." Shawn said with a slight smile.

"The carpenter," the Ranger said quietly. "I have heard the story also, I wish I had his character."

"As we all do," Traven said quietly.

It was quiet for a while then Traven looking at the lady asked, "Were you with the Wixon when Chamberlain was at the crossings?"

"I was," she said quietly.

"That was hell. We would all have been dead without you and the Wixon army." Traven said in a low voice. He looked at Tomlin. "Perhaps you should show more respect to the lady."

"I served under Heller, we ended the war." Tomlin responded arrogantly.

"Heller, he was a pet of King Jarrod. Heller should have had his head removed when he was with Beckett. I was at Dell when It was taken. Those men fought hard. I saw their women and children fight with their men. When we took the city, Beckett ordered all inside to be slaughtered."

A quiet fell over the group. The mention of the city of Dell was not only an embarrassment but a shame.

Paul stood up "I refused to kill children and women. I saw old ladies pulled from their houses and ran through with swords." He pulled his leather tunic over his head. The group looked in shock seeing scars on his back. "I received fifty lashes for not killing children." He put his tunic on and sat down. "I only remember thirty. It was Heller who swung the whip. He is a cowardly dog who always leads from the rear. We didn't win the war. We just stopped fighting. King Jarrod allowed King Axle to keep his realm. He should have been hanged. Paul was silent for some time then said "Heller is a cousin of the King.

Traven said "we have a hard day tomorrow, we need to rest." He looked at the big Ranger. "Would you like to tuck Tomlin in and tell him a story?"

The Ranger stood up taking the ladies hand helping her up. "I may rock him to sleep if I can find a big rock." He reached down, taking Micha's hand helping him up.

Chapter V

The wind was blowing hard as the camp was packed up. An hour's ride in the cold soon ended at the base of a steep trail. Traven stepped off his horse and with the reins in his hands led the horse up the trail. It was a difficult climb. Men fell as they struggled up the trail. Horses would slip and fall. The mules would often stop and refuse to go further. Micha would coax the animals up the trail. The wind picked up and with the cold it seemed to cut through them. It was miserable as the caravan inched its way up the steep mountain trail.

After five hours of strenuous work the group topped the mountain and began down the steep trail going down. After three hours of walking and pulling the animals Traven stopped at a wide spot on the trail.

He told the group there would be no fire for the evening. The temperature was dropping, it would be a long and cold night. The animals were bedded down close to the mountain wall. The wind had died down. Traven said he had seen several men watching them. They no doubt were waiting for them to stop for the night.

"We are not gonna wait for them to come to us in the night, or have them ambush us somewhere down the trail. We will hunt them down."

He told Aaron and Daren they were to take their bows and arrows and find a place to watch the camp. Micha and the lady would stay with the animals. The rest would come with him. The Ranger was reluctant to leave the lady alone but she told him Micha would be with her. He left with the other men.

Traven had the men spread out as they made their way across the rocky terrain. The moon was full and with the stars shining the men could see in the dim light. The wind was still blowing making it a cold night. Smoke was seen in the distance. The men headed for the campfire.

Men could be seen huddled around the fire. Traven set the archers on the north side. Speaking low he said "Archers will fire at the camp. They will retreat to the south and west. The east is blocked by the mountain. The Ranger with men will make their way to the west, I will take men to the south. The Archers will charge when the bandits retreat."

He was quiet as they all thought of the plan. It was dangerous and they were outnumbered. "No prisoners, they all die."

Paul felt the anxiety building up in him as he waited for the others to take their position. He knew it would be chaos. He stood up after half an hour saying "now, we all fire at once and then fire as fast as you can into the group."

The arrows were let loose and as they descended on the men at the fire the sound of men screaming could be heard. The arrows continued to rain down on the men as they panicked and ran. They were met by the big Ranger and his broadsword. Men fell under the sword. Many turned and ran as Traven leading his men met them in the dark. The archers with swords drawn hit them from behind as the fighting became more intense. The fight was soon chaotic and bloody.

The battle was over in a short while. Traven with others began to help those who had been hurt. Six of his men had been killed and all of them were wounded. The men started back toward their camp. No one spoke as they crossed the rocky trail.

Micha tended the animals as the lady stayed close to him. She looked up as she heard a scream. She saw a man fall with an arrow in his neck. Other men began running toward the animals. She told Micha to stay with the animals. She pulled her sword as a man ran straight for her.

Her sword clashed hard as the intruder brought his sword down. She stepped back and blocked his sword as he lunged at her. Another man was close, the man she was fighting was a good swordsman. Out of the corner of her eye she saw the man go down. Then another went down. She kicked the man in the knee which stunned him, then stabbed him in the chest. She immediately was in a fight with another man. She fell backwards as she scrambled to her feet she saw Micha with his sling striking men with rocks, other men were falling with arrows in them. She was sliced on her arm as she lunged stabbing the man in the throat. A man staggered to his feet. He had been hit with a rock she brought the sword up quickly, slicing his neck. Another man was swinging his sword as she jumped back. Her attention was on the man in front of her. Micha saw a man come up behind her his sword raised. He grasped the dagger and threw it. The dagger hit the man in the middle of the back. He staggered forward and fell. He was able to get up as the lady killed the man she was fighting. She turned to see the man get up. He died as she plunged her sword into his chest.

The lady grabbed Micha and moved behind a rock. Her heart was beating fast as she looked over the field. Men were laying dead. Some of them had arrows in them, others were bleeding from deep sword wounds. She saw a man get up, going to one knee. He rubbed his head as he looked around.

"Hit him with a rock Micha." She whispered.

Micha reached into his leather pouch taking out a rock. He stepped out from the rock twirling the sling. He released it, the man fell over backwards as the rock hit him in the forehead.

Traven stopped as he saw movement ahead of him. The men took cover. When the three men were close Traven stepped out with the others. The fight was over quickly as the three men died.

Looking down at the three bandits the Ranger suddenly started running down the trail. The others followed him. The Ranger entered the camp yelling, "Cassie, Cassie where are you!"

She stepped out from behind a large rock. "I'm here Reuban, Micha and I are alive."

He ran up to her breathing hard. He looked at the lady and closed his eyes "Thank you Lord."

Traven looked at the fallen men, he turned to Shawn, "find the others."

He walked to Mica patting him on the shoulder. "You okay, Micha."

With wide eyes he nodded his head. "Good, go check the stock." Traven said, smiling at the young boy. He watched Micha walk away.

Shawn returned shaking his head.

Traven started a fire as the men gathered around. It had been a hard fight and the loss was great. The lady put her blanket around Micha as she lay next to him. She put her arms around him as he silently wept.

It was cold and snowing as the men and lady mounted their horses and headed down the mountain early the following morning. The wind was blowing harder making it worse as it began to snow large fluffy flakes. They did not stop but continued to move down the trail throughout the cold bitter day. Traven did not stop as the snow began to pile up as evening came. It was dark as the clouds covered the moon and stars. He stepped down from his horse into snow to his calves. He led the horse as he trudged through the snow that swirled around him. The others also stepped off their horses leading them through the thick snow.

After several hours Traven placed his foot on the stirrup and swung into the saddle. The others did the same. Late into the night he stopped as the plains seemed to open up before him.

All of the men and woman stepped off their horses siff and cold. The animals were moved close together. The wind had died down as the snow was still falling. A fire was soon going as it crackled and popped with the wood being wet. Looking at the tired group Traven saying wearily, "we are through the narrow pass. It is open plains from here on out. We should reach Kachita in two days."

Chapter VI

The morning was clear and cold. The blankets were covered with snow. Micha felt the cold as he was up early. He looked back at the beautiful woman who lay sleeping. He had slept in her arms, her body warm against him. He loved her and decided he would do anything for her. No one had ever shown him love.

When the others woke a large fire was blazing. Reuben threw off the blanket, brushed the snow from him and walked to the fire. He smiled at Micha. "You did well Micha. I appreciate the fire."

Micha smiled as he handed the Ranger a warm cup of weak tea.

Traven was up as the others also made their way to the fire.

"The animals are fine, Traven. They came through the storm in good shape." Micha said as he handed the lady a cup of tea. She frowned as she sipped it. "It's licorice, sorry it's all we have left." He smiled, saying low. "It's from Traven's private stock."

Traven smiled broadly. "I don't mind sharing. Besides, it's good for you. My old Grandma used to give it to me when I was sick. It is my favorite tea."

Cassie looked at the brew. "Liquorice does have some medicinal purpose but it is not my favorite."

The men smiled as they sipped the strong brew.

The horses were saddled and with the sun shining with no wind it was a pleasant day. The group made good time through the snow that was high on the horses legs. The smaller donkeys struggled but the larger mules helped pull them through the snow.

On the second day late in the afternoon the group made their way slowly. The large city of Kachita could be seen. There had been twenty four that had started the journey now only six of the men with Micha who were worn out made it.

Traven stopped in front of a large tavern. He looked at Micha smiling.

"Little man would you take the horses and mules to the stable at the end of town. I'll get us a room and we can settle up with the lady."

Micha grinned. "That's what I do Traven."

All of them stepped down from their mounts as Micha gathered their reins.

"I'll give you a hand Micha," Paul said, taking the reins of horses.

Micha and Paul made their way to the stable as the others walked into the tavern.

Cassie walked up to the long counter with a woman dressed in a nice gown. The woman frowned at her.

"I require a room, a bath and my clothes to be cleaned."

The woman frowning said "I'm sorry but we do not allow Wixon to stay here. Perhaps you would be more comfortable across town where your kind stay."

Cassie reached into her purse and pulled out a small gold coin. She laid it on the counter. The woman was surprised. "If you do not show me to a room now, I will have your head removed."

The women watched as the large man pulled his sword and stepped forward.

"This way, I, I will show you to your room."

Cassie followed the woman up the stairs.

Traven and the men ordered supper. They all ate heartily. He looked at the young girl who brought him more water. "Would it be acceptable for my men and I to have a room?"

She nodded her head "of course, and may I recommend a bath as well."

Traven laughed as he ate. "I would think a bath would be good for all of us.

Cassie stripped off her clothes and stepped into the hot water. It felt great. She lay back thinking how it had been a hard trip. She knew it would be even more difficult when she went to the castle to confront King Axel.

The following morning the men sat quietly at a large table eating breakfast. Tomlin frowned. "When are we going to get paid? I want to go see the city and the lady is obviously sleeping late."

"Perhaps you should go wake her up." Micha said from the end of the table.

"Shut your mouth, runt." Tomlin growled.

"You shut your mouth Tomlin. I'm tired of hearing you complain. You can visit the whores all you want when the lady is ready to pay you. I suppose they can wait another few minutes for the treat you have to offer them." Traven leaned forward, staring hard at Tomlin. "You will get your silver when the lady is ready."

Tomlin stared back, looked down and ate his breakfast.

The men watched as Reuben walked down the staircase. He dropped a small leather pouch in front of each man. Tomlin immediately opened it and counted it. Reben glared at him. "The lady asks for your assistance. She wants to employ you for another mission."

"What would that be?" Tomlin asked.

"Does it matter?" Traven asked, placing the pouch in his purse.

Tomlin stood up and walked out of the tavern.

Paul stood up looking at Reuben, "I'll be drunk, when the lady needs me you come let me know I'll follow her." he walked to the counter and ordered a large tankard of rum.

Traven laughed, "Micha and I will be here when the lady is ready for us. I'm sure she needs good men to help you. I would hate to see you get hurt."

Reuben smiled, "Yeah, I'm sure she worries about me."

Shawn shrugged his shoulders, "I'm in."

The other men smiled and walked away.

Later that afternoon Traven sat at a large table looking down at the parchment paper and ink well. He held the quill pen tightly. Shawn walked over sitting down across from him. "Would you like some help?"

Traven looked up embarrassed. "I learned my letters but putting them together is always hard." he looked away.

My father was a valet to Adams in the old country. He taught me to write and work numbers. Then the war started and I was called off to fight under Hickman." Shawn grinned "I was in training to be a gentleman's gentleman."

Traven laughed, "I notice after you run someone through with your sword you always apologize."

"I see no reason to be rude." Shawn said defensively.

Traven handed the quill to Shawn as he picked up the inkwell and paper. Traven said "I'm writing to Beth. I'm sending her two silver pieces for her to travel here. I miss her and want her with me."

Cassie and Reuben sat next to Traven. A young girl brought a cup of tea sitting it down in front of Cassie. "Breakfast is lamb chops and potatoes."

Cassie nodded, holding up two fingers. She looked at Traven, "I will need you and the others in two days. I hope you will be available."

"Micha, Paul, Shawn and I will be ready to assist you my lady. Currently Shawn is busy with an important correspondence. He is my gentleman's gentleman."

Shawn looked up, "You don't know what a gentleman is Traven. You being the scoundrel you are." He looked at Cassie "I, my lady, was trained on an estate to be a gentleman."

Cassie smiled, "do you know math good sir."

Shawn smiled, "My lady has a sense of humor. Yes, I helped my father with the inventory of Mr. Adams estate."

Cassie dropped her smile, "I am glad to hear that Shawn. I have a job for you."

After several minutes Shawn sat the quill pen down and looked at the letter. He blew on the wet ink allowing it to dry. He handed it to Traven who looked at it. Cassy watched him then said, "may I read it?"

"Sure," he said quietly, handing the parchment to Cassie.

"Would you like to hear it Micha?" She said, smiling at him.

He grinned, "Yes."

My Dear Beth

I think of you often and miss you more than these words
can express. I am sending you two pieces of silver earned
from my recent journey. It was difficult but not as much as being
away from you my love. Please make haste and come to me here
in Kachitia. Be careful as you journey, I pray for you and safe
travels. I will see you when you arrive. Traven

Cassie smiled, "you are quite the wordsmith Shawn."

Traven took the letter and smiled saying "thank you. It was as if you were reading my mind."

The letter and silver were placed into a leather pouch with Beth's name placed on it. The inn at Solace was designated as where it was to go. Traven knew it would be a year and a half before she arrived.

Later that evening Shawn sat quietly in a large tavern across town. He knew it was where the Kings guard often visited. Since the war had ended the men had been sent to different regions to insure there was no trouble. The King's guard was a large force that protected the King and kept peace in the large city.

Shawn listened carefully as the men complained of the duty and not being paid. It had been four months since the men had received their wages. Their families were struggling and it was not fair. Shawn knew it was not uncommon for soldiers to complain. He was surprised that soldiers were not being paid. The men became drunker as the night wore on and the complaints became more bitter of the Captain of the Guard and lack of pay. There was anger in the ranks of the Kingsguard.

Chapter VII

Reuban Sent Micha to the livery stable to bring a carriage with two fine horses. Cassie had been out shopping during the week. Traven, Shawn, Paul along with Micha had stayed close to the Inn resting. They each had gone shopping replacing their old clothes. Each had invested their silver with money lenders. Their money would be safe and the investment would grow over time.

Tomlin had not been seen since he left for the brothel. They had been told they would need to accompany Cassie to the castle of King Axel. None of them smiled as they each thought of King Axel. He had started the war by attacking Kachita when King Benjamin Conrad had died suddenly. With the hard fought victory, he soon expanded the war which led to much bloodshed that had lasted seven years. King Jarrod agreed to a cease in hostilities and the war ended. King Axel was allowed to keep the kingdom he had conquered. Kachita was its capital. It was a bitter disappointment for all involved.

The men stood up as Cassie walked down the stairs. She was wearing an elegant white gown. She looked at the men asking, "Tomlin has chosen not to accompany us?"

Shawn said quietly, "Tomlin was at the brothel bragging of his latest adventure, and throwing silver around, he was found in his bed, dead."

Cassie shook her head, "I hate to hear that." She walked away as the others followed her outside to the waiting carriage. Reuben opened the door for her and taking her small hand helped her into the carriage. He stepped up to the driver seat next to Micha. Traven, Paul and Shawn stood on the back as the carriage moved through the crowded town towards the large castle.

The carriage stopped at the gate that was closed. Reuben stepped down walking to the guard. "Open the gate a Royal Lady has an appointment with King Axel." Reuben said in a loud voice.

The guard looked confused, as he spoke to another man. After a short discussion the gate was lifted up. Reuben returned to the carriage and drove through.

The carriage came to a stop in front of the castle Reuben stepped down saying,

"Stay with the carriage Micha."

He opened the door and helped Cassie step out. Traven, Shawn, and Paul followed Cassie and Reuben up the stone steps. When they reached the large doors where two men were stationed. Reuben stepped up hitting one of the men hard, he went down Immediately. Reuben hit the second man who also fell. He opened the door as Cassie walked in.

People in the Castle stopped and stared at the beautiful woman in the elegant gown followed by four men. She walked across the large open room to a set of doors that were closed. She stopped and looked at the two men.

"Open the door, I need to speak to King Axel."

"He has left orders not to disturb him, my lady," one of the men said smugly.

Reuben stepped around Cassie grabbing both men, throwing them across the floor. He walked back and opened the door. Cassie walked through it into the throne room.

King Axel was sitting on his throne. Several men were sitting on chairs in front of him. He was surprised as a beautiful woman in an elegant expensive gown walked in. He frowned Looking at the Captain of the guards.

"I told you I was not to be disturbed."

A large man with a protruding belly and thinning hair stepped forward. His face was red with rage. He raised his voice. "You are to leave immediately, or face death!"

The big Ranger pulled his sword walking towards the man. Shawn looked at Traven, and Paul. "I'm guessing this is where we are to be of assistance to the lady."

With swords drawn the three men followed Reuben. The Captain of the guard was shocked at the bold move. The men in the room on duty drew their swords and watched as the four men approached.

"Stop! Advance no further." The men stopped in front of the King's guard who stood with their backs against the wall, swords drawn. Cassie had raised her voice. She looked at King Axel who sat stunned.

"You will hear me King Axel or blood will flow."

King Axel looked at the beautiful dark-complected woman. He rose slowly.

"What is the meaning of this? You come into my throne room and threaten me."

She raised her head proudly looking at the man with contempt.

"I am Casandra Conrad, my Father was King Benjamin Conrad. You have usurped his throne. I am the legal heir of this realm. I have come to claim my throne."

A silence fell over the throne room. No one spoke, all eyes went to King Axel. Cassie turned walking toward the guards who stood against the wall with their swords drawn.

"I am the heir to the throne. This usurper has not paid you for months and your families suffer. Yet he has lavish parties for his nobles. Follow me and I will pay you all that is owed to you. If not you will die for an unjust King who sits on a throne that is not his.

Cassie turned and walked toward King Axel raising her voice, "You murdered King Benjamin and his Queen. You attacked and killed all the heirs to the throne, but not all of them. I was on Wixon island. You of course have no doubt destroyed the records of royalty so no one can claim to be an heir. Call for the Bishop. He will have records. The Pope will declare me Queen."

King Axel was stunned. "That is not possible, King Benjamin had no heirs, I defeated his army. I am King by my victory. I will not be intimidated by a halfbreed mongrel. Reuben walked quickly to the throne, He grabbed KIng Axel by the robes and threw him to the ground. The King staggered as he stood up. Reuben hit him hard, sending him crashing to the floor. He lay quiet.

Cassie looked at the men who sat stunned. "Send for the Bishop, tell him Casendra Conrad is here to claim the throne from this fake king." She walked to a man handing him a brown leather pouch. "Inside is a letter addressed to the Bishop. You will send a messenger to deliver it to him." The man stood up in shock. He looked at the men against the wall.

·   "William, take this correspondence to the Bishop."

A young man stepped away from the wall placing his sword in its sheath. He walked toward the man taking the leather pouch. He walked quickly toward the door.

Cassie looked around at the men who stood shocked. "Captain of the guard, pick this maggot up and take him to his room."

She walked to where the guards stood in shock. "Shawn, find the treasury and pay these men and all guards immediately. Also go over the ledgers they are keeping, I'm sure you will find some interesting bookkeeping. Take Traven and Paul, they can escort the men of the treasury to the dungeon.

"Aye my lady." Shawn looked at the King's guard. "Gentlemen please follow me."

She turned to see King Axel being carried away. She looked at the men who had remained, "gentlemen you are excused."

Reuben pulled the big broadsword and took a step toward the men. They all turned and ran from the throne room.

Cassie took a deep breath. She looked at the empty room. She walked out seeing men and women standing around whispering. She looked at an attractive woman who appeared to be older than her.

"I have decided to stay in the castle. Would you show me to a room?"

The woman nodded her head without speaking. Cassie followed her up the steps, Reuben followed her.

Chapter VIII

A young woman brought a pitcher of water and basin so Cassie could wash herself. She later brought her a platter of food. Micha had been sent to the inn to retrieve Cassie's clothes. He returned the carriage and walked back to the castle.

The following morning Cassie sent for Traven, Shawn, Micha, and Paul. She smiled brightly. "Today is market day. As a child I loved going with my Mother. I would like for you to go with me. I believe you will enjoy it." She looked at Reuben "would you like to come along? I believe you would enjoy the market." Reuben nodded his head slightly. "I'm sure there is a carriage in the barns. Micha would you bring one around."

Shawn smiled, I'll help him with the horses."

"I'll go with you," Paul said smiling.

Traven and Reuben followed Cassie down the staircase. She walked across the beautiful tile floor to the throne room. She waved her hand saying "open the door."

The young man opened the door as she walked in, seeing King Axel and other men in discussion. They all looked up as she walked toward them.

"I have sent for the Bishop. When he arrives he will have the documentation to prove I am Heir to the throne." no one spoke as they looked at the beautiful woman who stared at them with contempt. "I will be going to the market, and I will be using your carriage. Should you object, I understand. You may discuss it with my associates." She stepped behind Reubean and Traven.

"I have been speaking to your guard, your highness. They don't like you. They however, do appreciate my lady paying them their back wages. Also a bonus has been added to their pay. The money came from your treasury." Traven said as he stood looking at the man he hated. "Do you have any objections?"

"Traven." He turned and saw Cassie looking at him. She smiled slightly, "I am ready to go to the market."

He took a deep breath and glanced at Reuben who was staring at King Axel.

"I was hoping he had some courage and disagreed." Traven said frowning

"He's not a man." Reuben growled as his hand clenched his broadsword.

"We will be going now." Cassie said softly.

Cassie turned and walked out of the throne room. She walked out of the castle onto the large patio. She smiled as she saw a beautiful carriage with the king's seal on the door. She walked down the steps as Shawn opened the door taking her small hand. He helped her into the carriage and shut the door.

REUBEN STEPPED UP TO the driver's seat. Micha handed him the reins.

"No, Micha you drive the carriage."

Micha grinned, Slapping the reins on the horses backs. The carriage moved forward.

Micha stopped the carriage at the market which was at the west end of town. There were small tents and tables set up. Animals were in small pens. Men and women were walking through the market buying fresh fish, meat, vegetables along with pottery and jewelry. It appeared the market had everything.

The men and women stopped, being surprised to see the King's carriage. They all watched as a beautiful young woman with dark complexion and wavy long black hair wearing a beautiful blue gown stepped out of the carriage.

Cassie smiled as she walked through the market. Men and women bowed as she walked by. She pointed to a bench and said "Micha please ask that gentleman if I could borrow his bench."

Micha walked to the man who stood up. He handed the bench to the young man. He smiled nervously as he saw the men standing with her.

Holding Reuben's hand she stepped up onto the bench. She looked around as she saw a large crowd of men and women watching her. They all moved closer.

"I am Casandra Conrad. My Father was King Benjamin Conrad. Many of you will remember him. I am heir to the throne, his youngest daughter. I have sent for the Bishop and when he arrives I will be recognized as Queen." the crowd gasped as they looked at her. Many did remember King Benjamin. He had Married a Wixon princess, Myriam Kelly. They were all stunned.

Today I will enforce the old law that my Father established for market days. No taxes will be collected for those who sell or buy from the market. The usurper of the crown King Axel has abolished this law because of his greed. When I am Queen I will be fair to the people of this kingdom. No longer will Nobles take advantage of the people who they believe they are above." She stood quiet as the men and women began to talk with each other. She raised her voice. "Many of you may be nervous since I am half Wixon." She smiled "It is rumored Wixon practices magic, I assure you there is no such thing as magic. Do you suppose I can conjure up a dragon, or perhaps have a monster from the sea come and destroy Kachita. I am not a witch. I believe as you do in the savior Jesus Christ. Please do not allow ignorant superstitions to rule you. Put your faith in the Lord as I do."

She reached out her hand which Reuben grasped firmly as she stepped off the bench. Micha picked up the bench returning it to the man.

She would spend several hours at the Market walking through and seeing all the wares the people had to offer. Cassie was gracious to all the men and women in the market. She bought the men lunch then returned to the castle.

Nobles arrived at the castle to speak with King Axel. They were alarmed hearing an heir to the throne was now claiming the Kingdom. King Axel attempted to speak with Cassie who refused to speak to him. She had placed a large lock on the treasury door and had armed guards posted so no one could enter. Those who worked in the treasury remained in the dungeon.

King Axel with his captain of the royal guards approached the men of the Kingsguard ordering them to follow his direction since he was King. They refused to follow him. He attempted to speak with Traven, Shawn, and Paul. Traven laughed at him saying the kingdom was under new management. The king's guard would no longer recognize him since an heir to the throne would soon be in charge. The men of the Kingsguard had grown to hate King Axel and refused to follow him or the Captain. He was shocked his orders were disobeyed. When King Axel ordered his groomsman to saddle a horse the man simply turned and walked away. Paul who was at the stables did not smile as he looked at the King.

"You are not to leave the castle, you diseased dog. My lady has ordered you to stay. I regret she has also ordered no harm to come to you. I suggest you leave before I have to tell her a wild ass attacked you and stomped you to death. I would buy the ass a drink."

King Axel walked away with his fists clenched in rage.

Chapter IX

The Bishop arrived two weeks later. The Nobles were in an uproar as they demanded to speak to Cassie. She refused to see them. King Axel had attempted to leave but was told he could not leave. He was confined to his room with a guard on duty around the clock. The Kingsguard refused to follow his orders and when the Nobles had demanded they do their duty and protect the King, they were ignored.

Cassie stood on the patio as Bishop Connors carriage pulled into the castle courtyard. He was accompanied by a large number of men on horseback. They were his personal guard.

The Bishop walked up the stone steps and greeted her. She was wearing a white gown trimend in green. He walked up to her, taking her hand.

"You are Casandra Conrad."

She smiled brightly, "yes, your eminence. I have the west wing of the castle prepared for you and your men. You are most welcomed here."

"Thank you my dear. He placed his hand on her face, studying her. You favor your Mother my dear. I appreciate your hospitality. May I ask where King Axel is?"

"He is in his room. Axel has been a nuisance lately. I thought it would be best for you and your men to rest after your journey."

The Bishop laughed, "A nuisance? Well my dear I am happy he is not in the dungeon or dead. Axel has been many things over the years. Nuisance is one of the more polite names he has been called."

"Of course sir."

The Bishop turned and looked at Reuben. His eyes narrowed.

"May I ask good sir, you are a Ranger?"

"I am." Reuben said quietly.

The Bishop reached out, patting his arm. "It is an honor to meet you, my good man."

The Bishop was escorted to the west wing of the castle which was on the second level. When his luggage had been brought in Cassie said, "I have invited the Noble men of the kingdom to attend your hearing tomorrow. Should you not approve, I will inform them sir."

"No, my dear it is good you invited them. We will have an open and honest meeting, with no secrets."

Cassie frowned, "I have information here for you sir concerning the Nobles and their tithes. It is troubling." She handed the Bishop a large stack of papers. "Should you feel the need to verify the information? I will instruct the men guarding the treasury to allow you or your representative in."

LATER THAT EVENING King Axel walked to the west wing. He demanded to see the Bishop. He was denied and told to leave.

A small man approached the treasury door. He was a stern looking man. He cleared his throat. "I am Sanford Wills, the Bishop's representative of finance. I need to see the legers concerning the tithes paid to the church."

Shawn smiled, turned and opened the large lock. He opened the door and stepped back. Sanford walked into the room.

The following morning the Bishop walked into the throne room. It was crowded with men and women standing shoulder to shoulder. Cassie was sitting near the throne. King Axel was standing close to the raised platform the throne chair sat on. He had stated the throne was his and he would sit on it. Reuben told him If he sat on the throne he would die on it. He was visibly upset.

"I protest this action Bishop Connors, I have been treated as a criminal in my own throne room! I am the King!

Bishop Connors frowned as he sat down on a padded chair with a small table in front of him. "You are not recognized to speak Axel."

"This is ridiculous, I am the King recognized by the Pope!

The men and women in the crowd began to yell how unfair the King was being treated. They became louder as the anger and frustration was apparent. The Bishop's men moved in close to him.

The Bishop held up his hand. "If you continue to disrupt this meeting Axel you will be removed. If there is any more outburst, my men will clear this room. You were invited and are welcomed to stay. I will not tolerate chaos in this room."

The crowd grew quiet. King Axel was furious, but he stood quietly glaring at Cassie. Reuben standing behind her glared back at King Axel.

"We have before us a claim of an heir to the throne. The throne is currently occupied by King Axel. During a battle the Castle was defeated by Axel and his army. Since there were no heirs to the throne Axel became King. Now an heir has come forward to claim the throne." He looked at King Axel. "You are correct, the Pope has recognized you as King. He however did not crown you King. There has been no official coronation."

KIng Axel was stunned. "I am King. a coronation is not needed."

"A coronation has the Pope's blessing." Bishop Connors said firmly.

Bishop Connors stood up holding papers in his hand. He walked toward the men and women crowded in the throne room. "I have here legers from the treasury that indicate the tithes for the church have not been paid in full. My treasurer Sanford Wills has verified this with church records. Each of you who are delinquent on payment will give and account for your lack of faith." He looked at the Priest, "Father

Jacob please distribute these to the person indicated on the top of the paper."

Father Jacob took the papers looking at them then walked to men in the crowd and handed them to different individuals. When he was finished he walked back to the Bishop.

"You will collect the funds and send them to the Pope." Bishop Connors said firmly.

"Yes, I will." He said with his head down.

The Bishop walked back to his chair sitting down. He reached down and picked up several pieces of parchment papers that were yellow with age.

"The birth records of King Benjamin and his family. A young daughter born twenty seven years ago, Cassandra Conrad. She is the daughter of Queen Myriam Kelly, who was a Wixon princess."

The crowd was quiet and shocked as they looked at Cassie. She sat quietly with her hands folded.

"The child was born with her small toe and the fourth toe which grew together on her right foot. She has two webbed toes. The child has a birthmark on her neck that appears to be a small flower."

Cassie stood up walking to the Bishop. She removed her stocking and shoe. She placed her right foot on the table. The two small toes were webbed. She allowed the Bishop to look at her foot turned, around and unbuttoned her top button on her gown. She pulled it down and a birthmark was seen that looked like a flower. Cassie walked directly to King Axel. He stared down at her bare foot and saw the birthmark on her neck. He looked shocked. She walked back to her chair and put on her stocking and shoe.

The room was quiet. Bishop Connors said, raising his voice. "The church recognizes Casandra Conrad as the legitimate heir of King Benjamin."

The crowd erupted in anger. The Bishop's men immediately began to push men and women out of the room. The Kingsguard assisted them.

When the room was cleared. Bishop Connors said "You are not recognized Axel. Queen Casandra is, however, recognized by the church. Should you want to appeal this then you may seek the counsel of the Pope."

Cassie stood up, "You are banished from this kingdom. You will leave immediately. If you do not, or found on the grounds of this kingdom you will be hanged. I will allow you to have a mule to ride." She took a deep breath. "Micha, please saddle a mule and bring it to the front. Traven, please escort this person out of the throne room and see that he leaves immediately." She held her hand up, "no harm is to befall him."

TRAVEN WALKED TO AXEL grabbing his arm and dragging him toward the door.

"I, I'm the King. you can't do this!"

When they were outside on the patio, Traven threw Axel down the steps. He rolled down the steps landing on the dirt. He stood up shaken looking at Traven who glared at him with hatred. "I need my clothes, and money."

Micha brought a small mule around the corner. Traven stepped down the steps grabbing Axel and picking him up, throwing him on the mule. He stepped back and slapped the mule on his rump. The mule jumped and began running toward the gate. Axel hanging onto the reins tried to gain control of the running mule.

Inside the throne room Cassie ask, "Axel has left the castle?"

"Yes my lady. He seemed to be in a hurry to leave."

"And, is he okay?"

"Of course my lady. He did stumble as he went down the steps, but he is fine."

She raised her eyebrows looking at him. "Bishop, would you and your men join me for Supper? I do hope you stay for a while."

"Thank you my dear. I will be leaving in the morning. I will send a messenger to the Pope and will need to meet with him concerning your coronation."

Chapter X

Cassie sat next to Shawn looking at the papers in front of her. The legers showed how each of the Noblemen were not paying their full share of taxes. She sat back thinking, then said, "So Axel allowed the Noblemen of the Kingdom to not pay their fair share in taxes. No doubt earning their loyalty." She stood up, "Thank you Shawn, I will inform the Noblemen they are delinquent on their taxes." She smiled, "They did pay their tithes as required?"

"Yes they did, the Bishop is taking the tithes to the Pope. You know It was not easy going through the legers. I did the best I could but you should find a man who knows how to work the numbers well." Shawn said standing up.

Cassie smiled, "you did well." She kissed him on the cheek and walked out.

Traven and Shawn rode out of the castle the following morning with official letters for all Noblemen which indicated they were delinquent on their taxes. Each of them were ordered to report to the castle to meet with Queen Caseandra.

Riding out of town Shawn said "I am getting somewhat concerned with CC, she kissed me in the treasury."

Traven looked at him, "you're delusional. I swear you live in a fantasy world. CC is a lady and you are a rogue."

"I'm pretty sure she is in love with me. I mean really how can she not be, I am a fine figure of a man. She no doubt goes for the rugged handsome look." Shawn said seriously.

Traven turned to look at him "She kissed your cheek, didn't she."

"She kissed me. I'm pretty sure she is in love with me."

Traven laughed, "I'm pretty sure she is not." He laughed louder, "CC in love with you!"

"I'm pretty sure she is." Shawn said laughing.

They arrived at the first Estate. They stepped down from their horses and walked to the door. Knocking loudly at the door it was answered by an older man.

"We need to see your master Harris Culp." Traven said sternly.

"He does not want to be disturbed, sir."

Traven leaned forward saying low, "disturb him or I will."

The man walked away quickly. In a few minutes a finely dressed man asked "What is the meaning of this?"

Traven handed him the letter. He looked at it seeing it was official. His face turned red.

"I certainly do not owe back taxes!"

"Okay," Traven said as he stepped back. "Keep in mind if you do not attend the meeting Queen Casandra has scheduled for you. My associate and I will come and escort you to the castle. Have a good day sir."

"You did that very well Traven." Shawn said as they rode down the dusty road.

"No unnecessary bloodshed, broken bones. There may be hope for you as a gentleman."

"Just following orders, my good man." Traven said smiling.

Traveling across the kingdom Traven and Shawn would stop at an inn or pub talking to the common people. Cassie had asked as they delivered the notices of delinquent taxes they should stop and talk with people to see their reactions. Many of the men and women they met along the way were happy Axel was no longer King. They had been paying a heavy tax burden for years. They of course hoped a change in rulers would bring them some relief. Most did not think it would happen. All of the people hated Axel and the Nobles.

The letters would be delivered as ordered. Cassie told them she did not want any trouble. If the Noble was rude then they were to ride away and not kill anyone. There were few issues. It was as both had expected. When the Nobleman would receive their letter they became angry stating how they did not have to pay back taxes. Both men would smile and leave. Traven would inform them if they did not attend then they would be escorted to the castle.

The last estate belonged to Elias Waggoner. He stared at the letter, his face red with rage. "This is not right. I will not recognize that woman as Queen; she can't make me pay." He looked at Traven and Shawn sneering, "Go back to your illegitimate half breed female dog, tell her I won't pay her a copper!"

Traven hit the man hard in the face, he went down falling backwards. He looked at Shawn, "I pray he does not show up. I'll drag him to the castle behind my horse."

Shawn stepped into the room, seeing the man lay quiet. "He seems to be resting, We shouldn't bother his lordship."

Traven and Shawn returned to the castle after two months. They walked in seeing Micha dressed in a fine pair of red pants that went to his knees and long stockings with buckle shoes. His white shirt was pressed and a matching jacket. He wore a large round red hat.

Shawn grinned. "Micha they have gone and turned you into a gentleman."

Micha grinned. "I'm CC's valet. I'm learning to read and do my numbers. Reuben is teaching me the art of self defense."

Traven smiled, patting him on his shoulder. "I'm proud of you Micha. So just what does a valet do?"

"I announce visitors who want to see our Queen." Micha said grinning.

"Well then Micha would you announce that her two messenger boys have returned." Shawn said smiling.

Micha turned and walked to the throne room. He returned later saying "Queen Casandra says she will meet with you in the garden. It is such a lovely day she anticipates your company."

Traven laughed. "Lead on sir Valet."

Cassie was sitting on a stone bench looking at the garden. She smiled seeing Traven and Shawn. They sat down.

"How was your travels? I hope there were no accidents."

Traven told her of delivering the letters, and none of the noblemen were happy. Shawn reported some of their language was not christian. Also the common people were glad Axel was gone. The tax burden was tremendous. Traven added that they all have hope there will be some relief, However, most do not believe it will be much.

Cassie asked about the kingdom. She remembered as a child she and her family would often go to different parts of the kingdom throughout the years. Her Father believed it was important to see the people and speak to them. She was happy it went well. She frowned when Traven said there was an incident at the Waggoner estate. Shawn said Traven had insisted on manners and when the Nobleman didn't understand Traven explained it to him. Elias Waggoner now understands. Cassie informed them she was elevating Traven to Commander of the Army. Shawn would be second in command. Reuben would be her Captain of the Guard.

Later that evening Paul informed Traven and Shawn he was working with the army training archers. The army had been pretty well disbanded. New recruits were being brought in from the kingdom. Most were glad to be there since they were now getting regular meals. Many of the young men volunteered not wanting to work under the Noblemen of the kingdom. Traven said there was a lot of poverty in the kingdom due to the heavy taxes.

Micha came by the barracks telling how CC had spoken with the treasury men about working for her. The head man was dismissed. She told the other three she would allow them to work in the treasury; however, she would check their work regularly. Also she had cut the taxes for the common people by a third.

Reben joined them for supper. He still stayed close to Cassie but with the Kings guard now loyal he allowed them to watch over her. He also said "if something happened to her they would die, any family members they had would die, or any one they had ever talked with would die. A little motivation for the men." He continued, " I am told you will be commander of the army Traven, and Shawn has been placed in charge of the garden, I hope he can handle it"

"You know that's not right, I mean really the garden?"

"The army needs to eat, Shawn," Mica said laughing.

"See what a bad influence you are Reuben. Micah was a good kid." Shawn said, shaking his head.

"You can be the head cook and bottle washer." Traven said, looking serious.

"You guys need to get up off me, I mean it Shawn said frowning. "I'll tell CC and I no doubt am her favorite."

"Actually you being second in command can help keep Traven out of trouble." Reuben said smiling. "And by the way," Reuben said, holding up his hand, "CC? She is the Queen, I'm not sure calling her by her initials is appropriate."

The men laughed, "lighten up Reuben, you know we love her."

"Okay I suppose, but I do not want a nickname." Reuben said standing up.

"Let's go Micha, I don't want you hanging around this riff-raff picking up any bad habits."

Chapter XI

Casandra sat on her throne patiently waiting. Micha had told her the Nobles had arrived and were waiting to see her. She knew it was going to be a combative meeting. She did not wear a crown, although she had decided she would wear her Mothers small crown. Her Father's crown was larger and Axel had worn it. Casandra would wait until the Pope placed it on her head. With the Pope's blessing there would be no doubt she was Queen.

"Micha, please escort the Noblemen into the throne room." She glanced at the Kingsguard standing along the wall. She smiled knowing they were loyal. She had given them a bonus for their service. Reuben stood close to the platform the throne sat on top of.

Micha walked into the room followed by eight Noblemen. He bowed low and raised his voice. "The Noblemen of your Realm, my lady."

The room was silent as the Noblemen glared at the Queen. They were dressed in their finest clothes, each wearing a large hat. They were no doubt trying to impress her.

"There will be changes in the Kingdom. King Axel has been banished. I am the true heir to the crown and have been recognized by the Pope. He will inform me of the coronation. You will be expected to be in attendance. Whatever deal or arrangements you may have had with the usurper of the crown is now null and void."

She hesitated allowing the words to sink in. She could tell they were not pleased.

"The crown will now collect taxes from the people of this kingdom. You will no longer be required to collect taxes. A tax collector of my choosing will now be responsible for that duty. Each of you owe the crown back taxes, it will be paid."

"That's not happening!" Elias Waggoner yelled as he stepped forward.

"I collect taxes for the crown of my surfs. You half breed foreigner pretending to be Queen will not tell me how I run my region."

"Traven, please escort this gentleman to the dungeon." Cassie said calmly.

Traven walked quickly towards the man. He grabbed Waggoner who screamed,

"Remove your hands from me, you common dog. I am a Nobleman of birth!"

Eilis was dragged from the room protesting. Micha opened the door as Traven pushed him through. Micha shut the door as Waggoner could be heard yelling in pain.

Cassie sat up "You will pay your taxes or your lands will be confiscated. You no longer control the people of this kingdom. You collect above what is required and keep your share. If a farmer has had a harsh summer with little rain resulting in a failed crop, you demand the same payment as if the crop was good. No gentlemen, I, as Queen, will set the tax rate." She sat back taking a deep breath. She had to control the emotions raging inside her. "All of you push for war. Yet your son's did not serve. They were exempt. No longer. All eligible men will be conscripted into service. They will serve as any other man."

"Elite families have had their sons serve." Harold Reins said defensively.

"You were not recognized and will not speak unless I allow you the privilege. Serving as an aide to a Commander away from the battlefield is cowardly, and I will not have men of common birth slaughtered because of your egos." Cassie glared at the men who were stunned.

"Also know this, the law will apply to all men. Our law has been established from the bible. Any young man of an elite class forces himself on a woman will be hanged. The old tradition of elite privilege ends now."

Harold stepped forward, obviously upset. "Elite men have always had certain privileges. It is a practice that has been allowed for generations. Even during your Father's rein."

"He was wrong! I will not accept rape of a peasent woman to occur just because a young man feels he can because of his upper class." Cassie was furious. She stood up and looked at the Priest in the back. She walked towards him.

"Father, how is it acceptable to the Lord if a young man comes to confessional and confesses his sin of sexual immorality. Then returns, and confesses the same sin. How many times do you absolve him of his crime?"

The Priest looked nervous as he looked at the angry Queen..

"The confessional is a private matter and I am not going to divulge a confession. Not even to you my Queen."

"I did not ask for you to divulge a confession Father. My question is how many times do you absolve a rapist of sexual immorality if he continues to commit the crime?"

"I will not divulge a confession, it is private." The priest's face was red.

"Then I will ask the Pope when he arrives for my coronation." Cassie said, clenching her fists. She turned to look at the men. "I will hang any man who abuses a woman. The guilty man will not receive the benefit of meeting with the Priest before he is hanged."

"You can't do that!" Harold yelled.

"Shawn remove this man." Cassie said as she walked to her throne.

Harold was pushed and dragged out of the room. The others stood quietly watching the scene. They had never seen anyone treat them with such disrespect. The men looked at Cassie on the throne. Their world had changed.

She sat quietly staring at them. "I realize change is difficult, but understand gentlemen change has come. I will allow a certain amount of leniency as you and your families adapt to the new laws. You are dismissed."

Micha walked to the Noblemen. "Gentlemen," he said, gesturing with a wave of his hand.

The six Noblemen followed the young man out of the throne room. Cassie stood up and walked out of the room and ascended the stairs going to her room.

Cassie sat quietly in the dark cool room. She attempted to calm her mind as her emotions were raging. She despised the elite Nobles. She remembered as a child going to Lennox on the island of Wixon. She was a princess but many of the Noble families looked down on her since she was only half Wixon. Her skin was lighter and she had not been born on the island. Although polite she could see the contempt in their attitude. She had excelled in school. Her Mother had begun teaching her at a young age. She was further along in her studies than the others. Her teachers often mocked her which was humiliating. She had advanced quickly when she began to learn the art of war. Her ability with the bow and arrows, sword was superior to all her classmates, including the young men. When it was announced her Father had died, then the war had claimed her Mother and two brothers she was devastated. She had fought in an elite Wixon unit in the war. She had been a fierce fighter. She remembered arriving at the lower meadows where all of the Royal Rangers had been killed. The Wixon army had tracked the army of KIng Axel and engaged them. They all died. Being trained as a healer she had found Reuben alive. The other healers had told her he was too far gone. She stayed with him for over a year until he recovered.

She heard a knock on the door and saw it opened as a woman walked in carrying a platter. The woman smiled sitting the platter on a small table.

"Diner for you my lady." Barbara said, smiling. "Martha the head cook asked me to bring you food. I really don't want to go back and face her wrath if you refuse to eat. She can be difficult when upset."

Cassie walked to the table sitting down. "Well I certainly do not want Martha to be upset."

Barbara poured her a glass of wine. "Fresh fish with baked potatoes, and greens from the garden.'

"It is good. Please tell Marthat and the cooks I appreciate their efforts." Cassie said as she ate.

Barbara turned to leave, She heard "Please stay, I would like to speak with you." Cassie said as she wiped her mouth with a napkin.

Barbara was surprised the Queen had asked her to stay.

Cassie sipped her wine sitting the goblet down. "How are things in the castle with those who work here? I am curious."

Barbara looked at the beautiful woman sitting at a small table. No one of Noble birth or Royalty had ever spoken to her.

"Things are well my lady. Since King Axel has been removed we have all been paid and the bonus you allowed was appreciated." She smiled. "Of course Myria is not pleased. She shared the King's bed and was above the rest of us when he was here. She left going to her brother's house saying she would not stay with you."

"I'm sure there were other words she used," Cassie said, not smiling. She studied Barbara closely, who was a few years older than her being of medium size and thin. She was pretty with light brown hair. "What are your duties in the castle?"

"My Father was Chief Clerk to King Axel. I assisted him. He taught me how to write. As he grew older I did a lot of the correspondence for him. When he died, I assisted Harmon, who was the Clerk. He left when you arrived."

Cassie sat back. "I want you to be my Chief Clerk. I need a reliable person to take down notes and help me write correspondence."

Barbara was stunned. "A woman as Chief Clerk? I have never heard of a Clerk that was not a man."

"There is a first time for everything. You will be my Chief Clerk. In addition I want you to take control of the daily operations of the castle." She smiled, "except for Micha, he answers only to me."

Chapter XII

A week later Cassie sat on her throne looking at the tax records as Thomas Sands, her head treasurer, explained each realm and how much profit each had recorded. She looked up as Micha approached her.

"Yes Micha."

"My lady, a man wishes an audience with you. Greg Abbot a merchant from Seaside village."

Cassie looked at Thomas, "Seaside is on the coast. I believe that is Elias Waggoner's Realm.

"Yes, Your Highness. It is." Thomas responded.

"MIcha please allow Mr Abbot in."

Micha walked to the door opening it and walked outside. He walked in as a man followed him. Cassie was curious as she saw the man was nice looking tall and suntanned wearing nice but plain clothes. She smiled seeing Micha had stopped at the door as did the man. Micha motioned for the man to approach. He hesitantly walked toward the throne stopping well back. He went to one knee and bowed his head.

"Please rise, and come closer." Cassie said softly.

The man slowly rose and walked a few feet closer and stopped. Cassie smiled. "How may I be of assistance Mr. Abbot."

Greg looked down and cleared his voice. "I'm a merchant, your Highness, I, well I was chosen by other men who sail." He hesitated and looked down; he was nervous being in the presence of the Queen.

"Lord Waggoner is not available, and I, I was chosen to speak to you about the pirates that harass us constantly."

"Pirates," Cassie asked, leaning forward. There are pirates in our waters?"

"Yes they carry Letters of Mark, and raid our ships stealing our cargo." Greg was speaking just above a whisper.

"Letters of Mark, I have never heard of this. I do not know what that is."

Traven stepped forward, "My lady may I approach?"

"Of course Traven."

Traven stepped up close to Greg. "Letters of Mark is legal piracy. A monarch allows pirates to raid ships of an enemy. The pirates will keep a part of the loot and the kingdom will take the other part." He looked at Greg. "Did the piracy occur during the war?"

"Yes," Greg said quietly. "That is when it first began."

"And it continues?" Traven asked.

"Yes, the pirates are growing bolder. Lord Waggoner did speak to King Axel, who said there was a treaty with King Jarrod. The raiding of ships continues."

Cassie sat up. "King Jarrod is allowing piracy even with a treaty?"

"We cannot prove it your Highness. I am not accusing King Jarrod, but we believe the pirates are working with him."

Cassie walked to Greg taking his hand. "Thank you for informing me of this transgression. Traven, please show Mr. Abbot out and make him comfortable."

Traven walked with Greg to the back of the room and out the door. They walked out of the castle where Traven sat on the steps. Greg also sat down. Traven smiled at Greg. "You did well speaking to the Queen. You did seem a little nervous."

Greg smiled. "I admit I was terrified. Lord Waggoner should have been the one to speak to the Queen. Since he is locked up in her dungeon I was asked to speak for our village. I feared she would lock me up."

Traven patted him on the back. "I believe you will find her a different ruler than the arrogant Axel. I will speak to her, and I believe she will take action on this injustice."

"Thank you." Greg said standing up. "I will let the other merchants, and fishermen know we can expect help."

Traven walked into the castle and down the steps to the dungeon. Opening the door he removed the large keys hanging on the wall. He walked to the cell where he saw Elias Waggoner sitting on the floor. Traven let himself into the cell. Elias stood up as Traven walked in the cell.

"Does your Queen require you to beat me again?" Elias asked sarcastically.

"No, She doesn't ask me, I do that because I enjoy it. I have a question about Seaside and the pirates that are raiding ships. What do you know about that?"

Elias stared at Traven, "Letters of Mark were issued by King Jarrod to raid our ships during the war. After the war a treaty was signed, however, it continued. He is not an honorable man who refuses to honor a treaty. I spoke with King Axel. He asked the raiding to stop. But it did not. I went to King Jared's Kingdom but could not see him. I spoke to a smart talking treasury official, Damon Marks. He informed me that pirates were our problem."

Traven walked out of the cell and headed towards the throne room.

Cassie sat quietly listening as Traven explained what he had learned. She looked at Thomas "I imagine the raiding of ships has cut into profits of Lord Waggoner and the crown."

"Yes, it has had a tremendous effect. During the recent war it almost collapsed the economy. Lord Waggoner does have coal mines that enable him to still do quite well."

LATER CASSIE SAT IN her library and looked at Traven, "I want you to take men and travel to Seaside and find out what exactly is going on. Put a stop to pirates' raiding ships, and if you find any information the Pirates are working under the direction of King Jarrod I want to know."

Micha walked into the room carrying a cup and saucer. He sat it down on the table in front of Cassie.

"Thank you Micha."

Traven stood up. "I'll take Twenty men, and track down the pirates." He smiled looking at Micha, "I'll need good men so Micha you should come along."

Cassie sat her cup down waving her finger, "No, Micha is needed in the castle. Take Shawn with you so he can keep an eye on you so you don't get into any mischief."

Traven smiled as he walked off.

Three days later Traven and Shawn arrived in Seaside Village. He had placed the other men at Inns outside of the village not wanting it to be obvious the Queens guard was in the village.

Ellias and Harold were released from the dungeon and sent home.

Chapter XIII

Traven and Shawn split up as they reached the docks. Each of them walked around the docks talking to merchant men as well as sailors. They were all frustrated and angry that their cargo and fish were being taken by pirates. Traven spoke with Greg who said he was planning on leaving for Wixon Island in the morning with a large cargo. Traven told him during the early hours he would bring his men to the docks and have them aboard his ship. They would stay below deck. He believed there were no doubt spies who would inform the pirates of his cargo and his destination. He hoped to surprise the pirates if they tried to attack.

Early in the morning the Queen's guard crept aboard the large ship and went below deck. All of the men had experience on ships except Shawn. Their plan was simple when the pirates stopped the ship they would attack using surprise as their best offense.

Greg with his men set sail with the early tide. The ship had no problem as the wind was fair for the first two days. On the afternoon of the third day a ship was spotted heading for them. The ship pulled up beside the ship, threw grappling hooks and began pulling the ships closer together. Traven leading the men out of the bottom of the ship's hold charged the pirates. All of the men with swords in hand scrambled over to the pirate ship. The pirates were surprised and were overwhelmed. The battle was not long but it was intense. With most of the pirates dead, the remaining pirates gave up.

Traven had six men tied with their hands behind their back. The ropes cut into the mens wrist. Traven walked to an older man that was scowling at him.

"Where did you plan on meeting with King Jarrods men with the stolen cargo?"

The man spit on Traven's boot. Traven sighed and grabbed the man by the shoulders as Shawn grabbed his boots. They threw the man overboard. Traven walked to another man that was staring at him in shock.

"Where were you going to meet King Jarrods ship with the stolen cargo?"

"Bayside there is a deep cove that has a ship docked there to meet us."

Traven frowned at the men. He ordered the dead pirates to be thrown overboard, and the others to be taken below. He spoke with Greg and told him to go ahead and he would follow from a distance.

Greg approached Wixon island when he saw a ship heading for him. He looked back seeing Traven was closing in on his ship. When the pirates threw the grappling hooks on the ship Traven slowed and dropping anchor on the other side threw grappling hooks onto the ship bringing his ship in closer. The pirates, believing they had assistance, were surprised as they jumped onto Greg's ship; the Queens guard came over the rails and began fighting them. The battle was short and as it continued onto the other ship as the pirates fell back, it became more intense. Men from Gregs ship joined the fight and no pirate survived.

Greg sailed into port of the Wixon Island to sell his cargo. Traven stayed at sea with the two ships. His men asked to go ashore but he refused saying

"we're not here for tea with the Queen."

Both ships were searched thoroughly, a Letter of Mark was found on each ship.

After a week Greg's ship loaded with cargo from Wixon island sailed out of port. Traven on a ship and Manny Bonds on the other with limited crew trailed the cargo ship. The ships were a day from home when a ship was spotted. Traven and Manny both headed for the ship. The pirate ship was cut off from reaching Greg's ship. The two ships pulled up alongside and attacked. It was a fierce battle as the pirates fought back.

All of the pirates died in the battle and Traven lost three men. Six were wounded.

When Greg arrived in port the three ships docked outside the harbor. Shawn wrote a letter to Queen Casandra detailing the mission. Traven placed three Letters of Mark with King Jarrod's signature in a large leather pouch with the letter Shawn had written. He told Dalton Rhodes, "you need to ride hell bent for leather to the castle and deliver this to the Queen."

Dalton, a young man, smiled "It will reach the Queen."

He mounted a horse and was off in a cloud of dust. Traven recruited more men to accompany him in his quest to defeat the pirates. Many men volunteered wanting to be rid of the pirates. The offer of two pieces of silver was also a good incentive.

Dalton rode well into the night. He and his horse were exhausted as he stopped at a farmhouse. He pounded on the door until a man holding a candle opened the door looking at him through sleepy eyes. Dalton explained he was a messenger for the Queen and needed rest. The man's eyes were wide. He had Dalton come into his house. He woke up his son and daughter and had them put his horse in the barn where he was unsaddled and fed. Dalton was given a meal and laid on a mat near the fireplace.

The following morning water was brought so Dalton could clean himself. The two women scurried around the table as Dalton ate making sure his needs were taken care of. The older man walked in saying his horse had been fed and watered his son had saddled him and was waiting for him in the front yard. Dalton thanked the ladies and handed the man five copper coins. The man shook his head vigorously insisting he would take no pay for assisting the Queen's messenger. It was his family's honor. Dalton thanked the family and was soon on his way to the castle.

Dalton arrived late in the afternoon. He went immediately to the throne room. He smiled seeing Micha sitting in a chair snoozing. He shook MIcha gently. When Mica opened his eyes he said, "I have a message from Traven, I need to see the Queen."

Micha was on his feet going to the door leading into the throne room. He came out quickly saying, "She is anxious to see you Dalton."

Dalton followed Micha stopping in front of the throne.

"What news have you, Dalton?" Cassie asked anxiously.

Dalton handed the pouch to Micha who, seeing the pouch was covered in dust, opened it and handed the letters to Cassie. She took them and began reading. She looked up and handed one to Reuben. He looked up after a while and said in a low voice, "this is official Cassie. This gives pirates the right and privilege to raid ships from this Kingdom. Also there is no expiration date."

"Thank you Reuben," She said, "Dalton you look tired, how was your trip."

"It was good my lady. I stopped late at night and stayed with a family whose hospitality was very kind." Cassie smiled "I am pleased to hear that, go rest, you are no doubt tired from your journey." She walked into her library, shutting the door.

Cassie was furious. She took a deep breath letting it out slowly. She knew she would have to handle this situation delicately. King Jarrod still had a formidable army and hers was decimated. Even with the work to restore it there was no way she could stand against him. She picked up parchment paper and began to write to King Jarrod.

The following morning she asked Micha to have Dalton return to her throne room. She smiled at him. "I am sorry Dalton to ask you to return to Seaside so soon after your recent journey. I have a letter I need delivered to King Jarrod. Please find Traven and have him deliver it to The King." She stood up stepping off her throne. She walked toward Dalton. She handed him the letter.

"Please tell Tavern he is my messenger. I would hate for anything to befall King Jarrod. Please tell him to be on his best behavior."

Dalton smiled as he took the letter, placing it in a leather pouch. "I will relay your message my Lady."

"Also please give this to the family who was so kind to you. It is a gift and I want them to have it." She placed a small gold coin in Dalton's hand.

"I will my lady, with your compliments."

Dalton left the castle heading for Seaside. He stopped at the farmhouse seeing the family come out to greet him. He did not step down from his horse. He leaned over handing the man the gold coin.

"A gift from Queen Casandra, She was pleased with your hospitality. The family was shocked to see a gold coin which none of them had ever seen. Dalton smiled

"My compliments, good sir." He rode off quickly.

Traven was out to sea with the other ships. Dalton asked all the ships leaving that if they saw Traven he needed to see him urgently. Three days later Traven arrived at the Seaside docks.

Chapter XIV

Dalton grinned seeing Traven walk down the gangplank. He shook his hand,

"I have a message from the Queen." He handed the official letter to Traven. "She asks you to deliver this to King Jarrod. She also wanted you to be aware that you are her messenger and does not want anything to befall King Jarrod."

Shawn laughed. "So don't hit him or stab him, or throw him out a window."

"I'm a gentleman. I understand diplomacy." Traven said defensively.

Shawn continued to laugh, "No my friend you are a soldier warrior, no gentleman."

Traven smiled. "I have learned from you. Now give the men a break from their duties. I believe two weeks ashore would be appropriate." He looked around, frowning. "I don't understand why his Lordship Elias Waggoner allows the pirates he's hung to remain on poles rotting."

"Sending a message to all pirates I suppose." Shawn said, looking at the dozen men hanging."

"I suppose, Would you send a letter to CC and tell her of the latest developments with the pirates?" Traven said as he walked down the pier.

"It will be done good sir." Shawn said laughing.

Traven mounted his horse the following morning and headed for King Jarrods Kingdom. He was not in a hurry so he stopped and talked with several people as he journeyed. He would arrive three weeks later in the capital of the Kingdom.

It was mid morning as Traven approached the castle. The gate was open so he rode through seeing the courtyard had many people inside. He stopped his horse tying it to an old hitching post and walked up the steps. A young man in uniform looked at him asking "do you have an appointment sir."

"No, I have a message from Queen Casandra. I need to deliver it to the King."

The young man walked into the castle and returned holding the door.

"Come in sir."

Traven walked inside the large room seeing several people, an older man approached him frowning. "Who are you and what is it you want?"

"Traven Tisdale, I have a message from Queen Casandra for King Jarrod."

The man said bluntly, "hand it here I will take it to him."

Traven reached out, taking the man's shirt pulling him closer.

"Listen you rude little turd bug. You will take me to the King or I will gut you and throw your carcass in the courtyard to rot." He pushed the man hard and stepped toward him.

The man was shocked as he stared at the bigger man.

"I will not allow this kind of treatment." He stammered.

Two men in uniform walked up quickly.

"What is the meaning of this?" the older man demanded.

"Traven Tisdale I have a message from Queen Cassandra for the King. I will deliver it to his Highness myself."

The man looked at the other man who was obviously angry. He looked back at Traven.

"You will need an appointment."

"Then make one for me." Traven said, staring at the man.

The two men stared at each sizing each other up. Their hands on the swords. More soldiers appeared standing behind the older man.

"I was at the crossing with Chamberlain under King Jarrods banner. I see it is much the same, outnumbered. I suggest you gather more of your men if you plan on challenging me."

The older man smiled, "You were with Chamberlain."

"Yes I was." he eyes not leaving the man the man. "I have a letter from my lady who wants me to deliver it. She did not say exactly how it is to be delivered. I believe she will not be pleased if there is blood shed in King Jarrods castle."

"I don't believe King Jarrod would appreciate it either." The man said relaxing.

He walked to the angry man taking his arm.

"Theo, you will announce this man is waiting to see the King."

The man walked through a door then later walked out.

"The King says he will see you."

The older man standing next to Traven said, "Xavier Rawlings, Captain of the Kingsguard. No weapons allowed in the presence of the King."

Trven removed his sword then took out his dagger and handed it to Captain. Xavier smiled, as he handed the weapons to another soldier. "Follow me good sir."

Traven followed Xavier through the door. The room was crowded with men and women who were dressed in fine clothes and hats. Traven stopped in front of King Jarrod next to Xavier. He bowed low.

"I have a letter from Queen Casandra your Highness." He handed two letters to Xavier who walked to the King bowing and handing him the letters.

King Jarrod looked at Traven without looking at the letter.

"My steward says you were quite rude to him."

"I don't believe I was Sire. I explained to him that it was important I deliver my Queen's letter."

"You threatened him." King Jarrod said, frowning.

"I explained it to him perhaps a bit forcefully, not realizing he was so delicate."

Xavier laughed then caught himself. The King looked at him sternly. Xavier gathered himself.

"Sire, this man fought under your banner during the war. He served under Chamberlain. I ask you give some leniency to a soldier, who is not a diplomat."

King Jarrod looked at Traven. He sat back "tell me sir, we are all curious how Queen Casandra was able to take the throne from Axel. Did she have a large army? Some say she used magic."

Traven met the stare of the King. "There is no such thing as Magic as my Queen has explained many times. Only a superstitious fool would believe such gossip. She took the throne with four men and a young boy."

The King sat up, "four men, that is ridiculous. Axel had hundreds of men on duty. Please explain how she overthrew Axel with four men and a young boy."

"The young boy drove the carriage, myself and two other men and a Royal Ranger followed her into the throne room. Queen Casandra announced she was heir to the crown and Axel was a usurper. She told the men of the Kingsguard if they wanted to die for a corrupt King who refuses to pay them for their services, while he has lavish parties for the Nobles of the Kingdom, that was their choice. She said if they follow her she would pay them. So she paid them their back pay plus a bonus and she had Axel confined to his room. The Bishop arrived and confirmed she was the true heir to the crown. She is currently waiting for the Pope to crown her. I'm sure you will receive an invitation to the coronation, Sire."

King Jarrod sat back in his chair. It seemed to be an impossible tale.

"I hear Queen Casandra has been harsh on the Noblemen of her Realm. Why is that?"

Traven looked around at the men and women in the room. They were all watching him. He looked back at the King.

"Sire, the Noblemen have ensured taxes are collected from their surfs. Often they are harsh on collecting taxes owed to the crown and to themselves. The Noblemen have not paid their full taxes as the law requires. All are delinquent. Queen Casandra asks they pay what is required." He looked at the men and women then back to the King. "Queen Casandra has made it clear the law applies to all in her realm."

King Jarrod scanned the room looking at all the Nobles in his throne room. He smiled then sat back and began reading the letter. His brow increased with lines as he frowned. He looked up.

"Captain, please see that our guest is comfortable. I believe he would be more comfortable in the soldiers' barracks." King Jarrod stood up as all bowed. He walked off saying "Simon please come with me. A young man followed him out.

Traven followed Xavier out of the room. He could hear the men and women whispering. Xavier handed him his sword and dagger and walked out the doors onto the large patio. Traven leading his horse followed Xavier around to the back where his horse was put into the barn. He carried his satchel of clothes into a large barracks.

After he had cleaned up and changed clothes Xavier said "If you would like we can go visit Chamberlain. The old gentleman lives in the north part of the city."

"I would like that," Traven said.

The men walked through the city going through nice neighborhoods. The city was well kept and maintained. He had never been to the capitol and was impressed.

"The city has been revived since the war ended." Xavier said as they walked. "Now the south west part of the city closer to the dock is a bit rougher, with the seedier types who enjoy a drink or ladies who have a service you can pay for."

Traven did not smile. "Not much on drinking, or paying for love."

They arrived at a small cottage. Xavier knocked on the door. An elderly woman answered the door. She smiled, "Captain it is good to see you."

"Always a pleasure to see you Rene, is the old gentleman available. A former comrade is here to pay him a visit."

Rene smiled, "Yes of course he is in the garden relaxing. He will be pleased to have company."

The men followed her through the small house to the back yard. Allen Chamberlain looked up then slowly rose. He looked at Traven then smiled.

"Good to see you, my boy. Haven't been in any trouble have you?"

"Never sir," Traven said smiling.

The man laughed and invited them to sit down as Rene bought them a cup of tea. They would stay and have supper talking of the war and what was going on in the world. Chamberlain laughed as Traven told him of Cassie. The trip over the mountains with Reuben, the last of the Royal Rangers. When it was late they left the cottage.

Traven would sit up with the men of the Kingsguard talking until it was late in the night.

Chapter XV

King Jarrod sat quietly as Simon, his youngest son, read the letter. Simon sat it down and looked at the Letter of Mark. He looked at his Father not speaking. The door opened as Damon Marks, the head Treasurer walked into the room. Simon handed him the two letters. Damon read the letter from the Queen then looked at the Letter of Mark.

King Jarrod leaned forward, his anger in his eyes flashing. "How is it that the Letter of Mark with my signature was taken from a pirate ship when I signed a treaty ending piracy?"

Damon was scared. "Your Highness, the war was costly, we paid for it through the pirates raiding the enemy. We have been able to rebuild your Realm by having our former enemies pay for starting the war."

"So my word means nothing! My signature on a treaty stopping privacy is worthless since this kingdom continues to hire pirates!" King Jarrod said, slamming his fist on the table.

"No, no your Highness, I was only ensuring the kingdom was paid back for all the money spent on the war."

King Jarrod looked at Simon. "Draft a letter ending all piracy. It is illegal in this kingdom to associate with pirates. Any person who participates in piracy will be executed." He sat back looking at Damon, he looked at Simon. "Also write a letter to Queen Casandra and try to clean up this mess."

"Aye, Sire," Simon said, walking to a small table picking up parchment paper.

"Tell me Damon," King Jarrod asked in a controlled voice. "How many of the Noblemen of this realm are behind on their taxes?"

"I'm not sure Sire, I can certainly look. I can have my people gather the information for you." Damon whispered.

"You do that, then you check their numbers, then I want you to explain it to Simon. He will bring it to me."

Damon glanced at the young man behind the desk writing. He knew Simon was intelligent. The Queen had lost two sons in the war, and one was wounded severely. He had recovered but had come close to death. She refused to allow her youngest son to be in the war. She had him study with tutors, learning rather than fighting. Simon was brilliant. Damon looked at the King, "may I ask why you want to know about the Noblemen's taxes?"

KIng Jarrod leaned forward, "no, as King I do not have to explain to you why I issue an order."

"I was not supposing anything Sire, only curious." Damon said looking down.

"Simon will be in the treasury in the morning to look at your reports." King Jarrod said, staring at Damon. "Leave me," he said sternly.

Damon walked out quickly.

By mid morning Simon walked into the King's private study. King Jarrod sat back "I like your letter, you have a way with words. I believe the Queen will see through the excuses, so I want you to deliver it to her yourself." He looked at Simon, "I understand she is a beautiful woman. You need to remember you represent this kingdom. Do not allow her beauty to distract you from your mission."

"And exactly what is my mission, Father."

"To clean up this mess. Convince her we are allies. I hated Axel. The war was costly in human lives and money. I realize many are angry I did not force Axle out. I allowed him to keep his small kingdom to stop the war. How many more men needed to die. It would have been a long drawn out campaign. The cost of lives would have been tremendous."

Simon sat down and explained that all the Noblemen were behind in their taxes. Some of them owed a tremendous amount. The King frowned, not happy with the report.

Damon was called before the King and tried to explain he had been lenient on the Nobles. King Jarred Instructed him to draft a letter with the amount owed to the crown and deliver it himself. He would be escorted to the estates of Noblemen by the Kingsguard.

Late in the evening King Jarrod met with Xavier asking about Traven. Xavier looking at the King said, "this man is the real deal. He is loyal to Queen Casandra."

He told the King of Traven leading her and a group of men across the Mountains, the battles they faced. About Reuben the Royal Ranger and how they had boldly walked into the throne room and taken the Kingdom. He said "according to Traven, Queen Casandra is the most beautiful woman he has ever seen. She is not only smart, she is cunning, and a warrior, who has compassion."

King Jarred slowly stood up "talk with Traven, tell him I will be sending Simon to deliver my letter of response to his Queen. Simon is his Mother's favorite and I ask him to protect my son."

Traven stayed at the castle for five days. He walked around the city seeing the sights. He rode out into the countryside seeing farms with crops. Cattle, sheep, and goats, in the fields, along with herds of pigs. He was impressed how the people had responded after the war. It was much the same as in his new home. He often thought of Beth hoping she would soon arrive. He had talked with Greg as well as other merchants and fishermen to watch for a ship that would be arriving from Stirling which would be the port she would leave from. He was anxious to see her.

It was early and Traven was anxious to be on his way. He stood patiently holding his horse's reins as Simon's mother hugged him goodbye. She talked to him in low tones and was weeping. The King said gently, "It is time for you to be on your journey Simon."

Simon walked down the steps and mounted his horse as Traven did the same. He waved as tears ran down his mothers cheeks. They rode out of the castle and through the town. When they reached the open plains Traven looked at Simon.

"So what am I to call you Prince?"

"You can call me Simon, that is my name." Looking at Traven he said "I've noticed you have a way of speaking that sounds respectful, but has a little sarcasm."

"Habit I suppose. Does it bother you Prince?"

"Just call me Simon. Yes it does bother me. I'm not sure you have little respect for authority, or because I did not fight in the war."

Traven did not smile as he looked ahead. "Respect is earned, it's not something that you are born with as most Nobles believe. I respect the men who did not fight in the war since they stayed home and raised crops, livestock so we could eat. Men who worked in mines to dig coal so families could be warm. Merchants who carried supplies to the lines. They did their part. You have to earn respect, Prince."

"Will you stop calling me Prince?" Simon asked.

"Probably not," Traven said flatly.

The day soon became hot as the two men traveled. Neither spoke as they watched men and women in the fields. Many of the people who passed knew Simon was the King's son. They stopped and bowed to him. He would nod, wave and continue. He would glance at Traven who had no reaction. They stopped in the evening at an Inn. The people of the village were excited to see Simon.

The days would continue as the men traveled. Approaching the border Traven stopped at mid day and said "step off your horse." Simon was confused as he stepped down. "Walk on the other side of your horse" he said urgently.

Simon compiled without arguing. He saw several men on the road. Traven walked ahead of Simon looking directly at the men. A large man smiled

"Welcome my fine gentlemen, it is good to have you in our fair country. This is the King's road and I am his collector of tolls."

Traven did not speak as he approached the men. When he was close he pulled his sword and lunged forward stabbing the man in the chest. He immediately began fighting with another man. Simon stepped up and engaged a man. Traven stepped close to Simon as he fought with another man. Simon stabbed the man in the throat and was immediately fighting with another man. Traven killed the man he was fighting then stabbed the man Simon was fighting in the neck, he fell face first.

Traven mounted his horse and began riding at a galloup. Simon was behind him, his head spinning. He had been trained to use the sword and dagger. He knew self defense. He had never killed a man in combat. He continued to ride following Traven. He was surprised when Traven came to a village but did not stop. They continued to ride well into the night.

Simon was exhausted. When Traven stopped at a farm house. He did not knock on the door but went into the barn. He shut the door behind him and lit a candle he found on a large box. They unsaddled their horses and rubbed them down since the horses were perspiring with a heavy lather. Traven found grain and fed the horses as well as giving them water. He laid down in a stall going to sleep. Simon wondered why not knock on the door and sleep in a bed. He lay down and was soon asleep.

It seemed Simon had just closed his eyes as Traven was shaking him telling him to get up. Simon stood up wearily and began saddling his horse. Traven opened the door and both men walked out holding their horses reins. They were soon mounted and riding in the moonlight. Traven did not stop until it was late evening. He finally stopped at a farm house and asked if he could spend the night. He told the people he was the Queen's messenger. The old man looked gruffly at the men and said "You're welcome to stay in the barn."

Traven thanked the man and walked to the barn. An older woman came into the barn bringing them a biscuit and some bacon. Traven gave her four copper coins. She granted and walked out.

Traven laid in the hay loft. "Most people have lost sons, husbands, relatives in the war. They don't like royalty."

"We are in Queen Casandra's country are we not?"

"Yes," Traven said, yawning, we crossed the border about an hour ago."

Chapter XVI

A day's travel they saw a large estate. It was well maintained with many people working in the fields. Traven stopped at the front of the estate seeing an older man and woman glaring at him.

"Ride on, you are not welcome here." The man said gruffly

Traven walked his horse to a large wooden trough full of water. He stepped off allowing his horse to drink. Simon stepped off hearing the man raise his voice.

"I said ride on, I do not want you on my property."

"Or what?" Traven said, stepping toward the couple. He saw six men looking at him. They were armed with swords and daggers. He stepped closer toward the men.

"I'm Traven Tisdale, Commander of Queen Casandra's armies. I'm on a mission and returning from KIng Jarrod's Realm. I don't want trouble." He pulled his sword, "but I will not back away from it."

The men did not move.

"I don't care who you are!" The woman screeched. You are to leave now! Go back to your mongrel Queen." She said, spitting on the ground.

"I'll be happy to pass your message along." Traven said, staring at the woman. He turned and looked at the men.

"So who will follow this braying ass who commands you. Please gentlemen, I invite you to try."

None of the men moved. They were well aware of who he was. They could see the other man with his hand on his sword.

Traven and Simon mounted their horses. He looked at the man and woman.

"I pray you soon die a painful death, crapping all over yourselves in agony. I will be overjoyed to here of your demise knowing you will both be in hell being raped by deamons."

Simon did not speak to Traven as they rode along the dusty road. Traven pointed to a village. "Dell, I'm sure you recognize the name."

Simon nodded his head remembering how all in the town had been slaughtered.

Riding through he saw the town was larger than he had imagined. Most of the houses and buildings were vacant. Only a few people were in the village.

Traven did not stop but continued. He said quietly as they rode out of town

"The Noble Family Sampras were killed along with the villagers. Axel allowed the Hocking family to move in and take control. King Jarrod did send funds to Axle for the tragedy. Axel kept a large part, and Hocking kept the rest. No funds were given to the pheasants. Not surprising the action of royalty and Noblemen behavior."

Simon started to argue but chose not to push the point.

Only a few fields were being worked with crops in the fields and animals being raised. Many of the fields were bare, having weeds growing on the unattended fields.

It would take another week for Traven and Simon to cross the realm. The war had taken a toll on the inhabitants, but as human nature is resilient the people had begun to rebuild. Farms, with crops, and animals were seen from the road. Traven did not speak much but if Simon would ask a question he would answer him.

They arrived at the castle in the late afternoon. A young man smiled as he grasped the reins to the horses, taking them to the groomsman. Traven saw Micha at the door smiling. "How was the trip, Traven?" He asked excitedly.

"Good, all is well my friend." Traven said as he walked up the steps.

"CC is anxious to see you," He looked at the other man. "May I ask your name sir. I will announce you to Queen Casandra." Mica said, looking at the man with Traven.

"I am Simon Shea, King Jarred's son and ambassador."

Traven walked to a table with a pitcher and a large water bowl. He poured water into the bowl and began washing the dust off. Simon followed him and also wanted to clean up before meeting the Queen. A young woman walked to them smiling,

"Welcome home Traven." Laying towels on the table.

"Thank you Lou Ann, it's good to be home." Traven said as he dried his face.

Simon said as he washed his face and neck. "The young boy is the Queen's steward?"

"Yes," Traven said "Is that a problem Prince."

"I was just surprised since most Stewards are older. He appears to be quite young."

"Micha has earned his position. He is a favorite of the Queen."

Simon dried his face and neck, saying "Like a pet."

Traven stepped toward Simon and grasped his neck with a strong hand. The vice-like grip of his fingers closed around his neck.

"That young man has earned the respect of my Lady, and men of this castle. Respect has to be earned, not something born to Royalty, and Noble men. You will not disrespect him."

"Traven!" Micha said, raising his voice. "I, I believe the Queen would like to talk to him."

Traven relaxed his grip. He stared at Simon. "Be careful of your tongue or I will rip it out of your smart Royal mouth." His eyes were blazing in anger.

"I apologize, sir." Simon gasped

Micha turned and walked into the throne room. Traven close behind Simon who followed Micha. Simon was surprised there were few people in the throne room. He heard The young man say Prince Simon Shea, son of King Jarrod, and ambassador." he looked nervously at Traven. "Commander of your Majesties Armies Traven Tisdale."

Cassie knew there was a problem seeing the anger on Travens face. She saw the fresh red marks on Simon's neck. She stood up walking toward Traven. Reuben followed. She smiled, "It is good to have you home Traven. You look tired and I'm sure you have other duties to attend to, we will speak later."

Traven took a deep breath, "Thank you my lady. I will be available when you are ready to see me." He turned slowly glaring at Simon walking past him.

Cassie walked back to her throne. She smiled slightly. "You are welcome here good sir." She had intentionally not acknowledged his royal status. It did not go unnoticed. Simon picked up on the breach of protocol.

He smiled, still shaken from the attack. "My father the King sends his regards and well wishes to your Highness. I carry a message from the King he asks I deliver to you."

He looked at Micha and started to hand it to him then hesitated. He looked at Cassie. "Queen Casandra, I recently insulted Commander Tisdale and want to extend my apologies to not only him, but to you." he bowed low then handed the letter in a sealed envelope to Micha.

Micha walked to Cassie, bowed, and handed her the letter. He turned and walked to the back standing by the door. Cassie stared at Simon who looked back at her. She did not open the letter, instead tapped it on the arm of the chair.

"How are things in your country Simon?" She asked.

"Going very well, your Highness. The people are rebuilding as I have observed here as well. The war has been costly to both sides."

Cassie smiled knowing Simon was eloquent. He was also very intelligent."

"How was your trip? I realize Traven can be a rogue at times."

She had made him uncomfortable.

"It was a good trip. We were accosted by thugs inside my Father's Kingdom. We were able to defend ourselves and prevail. Traven is a mighty warrior. I believe you are wise to choose him as Commander of your armies."

"I'm glad you were able to prevail on your perilous journey." She stood up

"You must be tired. Micha please escort the Prince out, and have Lou Ann take him to a guest room."

Simon bowed and followed Micha out.

Chapter XVII

The following afternoon, Reuben followed Cassie to the soldiers barracks. She walked in and all the men immediately came to attention. She smiled, waving her hand. "Only a social visit men. Please carry on."

She walked to the back room where Traven and Shawn stayed. She opened the door seeing Traven, Shawn and Paul sitting at a table playing cards. They immediately stood up. She smiled "whose winning?"

Paul smiled, it was obvious he had been drinking. "I'm giving these two gentlemen a lesson in the art of card playing my lady." He said bowing low.

Cassie walked up to him looking at him, "How are you feeling Paul? You don't look well."

"Fine my lady. I feel so good I may take Reuben out and challenge him to a wrestling match."

"I'm not sure that would be wise Paul. I don't want to see Reuben hurt."

She sat down "Now then Traven tell me of your adventure."

Traven shrugged his shoulders, "not much to tell my lady. I delivered your letter. King Jarrod was curious how you were able to take the throne, and why you were treating the Nobles so harshly."

"What was your answer?" She asked as she leaned back.

"I told him the truth.

"What were your impressions of my kingdom?"

"Poor shape. His Lordship Hocking and his chubby wife have done nothing to rebuild Dell or the land. He is a self indulgent pig." He sat quietly trying to control his emotions. "The other parts of your realm are rebuilding slowly. The large estates of the Nobles are doing great since they insist on gorging themselves on the labor of Surfs and giving very little back."

Shawn leaned forward. "Now Commander don't hold back, Queen Casandra wants you to tell her what's going on.?"

"You're demoted to cleaning stalls, smartmouth." Traven said glaring at Shawn.

"Now commander, don't be bashful, speak up." Paul said grinning.

"You are now his assistant." Traven said, leaning forward.

Cassie laughed. "Alright, stop it. I believe I have the information I need." She sighed "It is as I feared. "I am having Barbara draft letters to go out to the realm inviting all veterans that have fallen on hard times to travel to Dell for an opportunity. The crown will fund businesses to start up."

Shawn's eyes narrowed. "My lady with respect, some of the veterans have turned to outlawing as their trade. I would suggest caution."

"I agree," Traven said. There will be many who respond who will want to start over. I don't have a lot of confidence in Hocking. He will take a large portion for himself."

"I am working through the details. I will not announce this for a while."

Cassie stayed and talked with them for a while then she and Ruben left

.

The following day Shawn stood silently watching the young men practicing with their bow and arrows. John Stuts standing beside Shawn said sarcastically,

"well it is good to have you make an appearance Paul."

Shawn saw Paul walking towards them it was mid morning. He looked bad. His complexion was pale with a slight yellow tint. Paul ignored him and walked up the line of young boys. He stopped and gave advice to help a young man.

John frowning watched him. "Nothing but a rummy, I don't know why the Queen won't dismiss him. He's useless."

"Be careful how you speak Stuts. That man has more experience with a bow than any man I know." Shawn said, turning to face John.

John had fought under King Axel, he was allowed to stay by swearing his loyalty to Queen Casandra. He had grown to hate King Axel.

"He's a falling down drunk. We all served and saw hell. You're making excuses for the man."

Anger boiled inside Shawn. He took a deep breath, "I don't make excuses for any man. The war is over and I hold no grudges for any man who chose to fight on the side he felt conviction. Paul was at Dell. He witnessed the worst of humanity, and he refused to participate. He bears the scars of fifty latches for his convictions. He drinks to numb the pain. You and I killed many men in the war. The difference was they were men in combat. Not women and children." Shawn paused. He continued to look at John. "How 'bout you John, when a village was taken did you rape the women who survived. That's part of the deal isn't it. The women are the victory celebration. How many women did you hear screaming and crying as you took them?"

The two men stared at each other when John looked away saying "too many."

Simon had asked to speak with Cassie as the days passed. She had refused to see him. He was sitting on a stone bench in the garden watching the women and young children tending to the vegetables.

Simon was surprised as Cassie walked out and sat next to him. She smiled.

"I love the garden. It is peaceful out here."

"Yes it is," he said, watching her. "I have been wanting to speak to you. I am glad you have finally allowed me the opportunity."

"You are very elegant. Perhaps you should speak plainly, and not try to impress with your extensive vocabulary." Cassie said, looking directly at Simon.

"Do I offend you Queen Casandra?" Simon asked politely. "Is that why you refuse to see me?"

"Yes, I am offended. King Jarrod did not take any responsibility for the raiding of ships after he signed the treaty. He made excuses, and offered no apology."

"He was not aware the head of the treasury had chosen to continue the raiding. When it was brought to his attention he stopped it immediately. He has offered compensation." Simon had raised his voice irritated.

Cassie continues looking him in the eye. "Raise your voice to me again and I will send your head back to your Father."

She stood up and walked away.

The following morning Simon was told he was invited to the throne room as Queen Casandra was holding meetings with each Noble family. When he arrived there were a large number of people who were in attendance in the room. Micha escorted him to a seat that was close to the throne. He was surprised to see a woman sitting at the table the Chief Clerk sat at.

Each Nobleman was called. He watched as Micha walked in with the Nobleman following. He would bow and announce the man. Simon was impressed with the young man. He saw on the opposite wall the Kingsguard as well as Traven.

The Noblemen were given the opportunity to speak. All of them had excuses as to why they were delinquent on their taxes. The high cost of the war. Pirates, and bandits attacking them. Queen Casandra sat quietly and each time said the same thing to each one. "I will accept no excuses. You will pay what is owed to the crown or your lands will be confiscated. You will not be allowed to impose heavier taxes on Surfs so you don't have to bear the burden of a problem you created."

The Noblemen would agree and arrangements were made for the payment.

Lester Hocking was the last Nobleman to be called forward. He was arrogant as he approached the throne. He did not bow as expected. He nodded his head slightly smirking at The Queen. As he started to speak Cassie held up her hand. She stared at him. "Mr. Hocking, your debt to the Crown is tremendous. You, unlike the other Noblemen of this Kingdom have made no effort to repay the taxes owed. You have also taken the money King Jarrod sent in reparations for the tragedy at Dell, and kept it for your own selfish desires. There has been no attempt to rebuild the lands under your jurisdiction and authority. Please explain why I should not have you hanged."

Hockings was shocked. "I am a Nobleman by birth. I will not be spoken to like this by a half breed. King Axel is the legitimate King you madam are a pretender."

Cassie leaned forward, cutting him off. "Your lands are confiscated by the crown and you will stand trial for corruption. You will be given an opportunity to defend yourself by a jury of your peers." She looked at Traven. "Take him to the dungeon."

Linda Hocking was on her feet screaming obscenities insisting she had no authority to speak to a Nobleman in such a manner. Traven had Lester by the arm. He walked past Linda grabbing her by the arm and throwing her across the room. Shawn walked quickly up to her, picking her up and dragging her out of the throne room. Both were locked up in separate cells.

Cassie stood up. "There will be a trial where each of the Noblemen will be in attendance. All of you are dismissed." Cassie walked to her private library and shut the door.

Chapter XVIII

Cassie sat quietly in the dimly lit room. She was angry and knew she needed to be careful. She was aware the other kingdoms were no doubt monitoring her. Their systems for generations had been built on Nobles running large areas of a kingdom. Surfs served under them. She hated the system, but knew if she disbanded the Nobles the Nobles in other kingdoms would see it as a threat to their culture. There would no doubt be another war.

She heard the door opening and watched Barbara walk in, sitting a cup of tea with a saucer on her small table. Barbara smiled and said softly, "Horehound tea, it will help sooth your emotions."

Cassie smiled, "thank you Barbara. Please sit for a while."

Barbara sat down as Cassie sipped her tea.

"You grew up in the castle. I remember you when I was young. Your Father was Arther Cravens."

"Yes your Highness, I worked closely with him."

They both sat quietly in the dark room. "I want you and Shawn to travel to Dell and set up the town. It is important we establish the town with people who will no doubt be intrigued by the recent announcement asking for settlers. You will assign the homes and lands to all who are interested in settling in the community." Cassie smiled slightly sitting her cup down on the saucer. "You don't have any problems working with Shawn, do you?"

Barbara was surprised, her cheeks red. She and Shawn had been together for some time. "I believe working with Shawn will be an asset." Barbara said softly.

"Good you will leave in two days." Cassie said, picking up her cup.

Shawn and Barbara arrived in the vacant village of Dell two weeks later. They walked through the village seeing it was overgrown with weeds and animals. The houses were in good shape. They both sat outside of a large building. They watched as men walked into the village approaching them. The six men stopped in front of them. Their hair was long and unkept. Their beards were long and shaggy. A large man stepped up as Shawn stood up.

He held up a piece of parchment paper. "This says land and homes for those who want to settle in this village."

Shawn smiled. "Queen Cassandra wants this area of the kingdom to be populated. We are all aware of what happened here. She is offering to help any who choose to move into the village with money to start up their business, or land to plant crops or raise animals."

Men and women walked up as Shawn was speaking. He looked at them all.

"It is simple, men and women move in and begin producing products, crops, raising livestock, in order to restore the land. People make money and they pay taxes. The taxes have been reduced so her subjects will be able to keep more for themselves."

"What about the Lord, the Noble family will take a large share of our work."

A Large man snarled who was obviously suspicious.

"Hocking and his wife are in the Queens dungeon." Barbara said standing up, walking up beside Shawn. "I'm sure a Noble family will be assigned. Taxes will be collected by the person chosen by the Queen. The Noble family will be in charge of the area, but there are now limitations.

"I'm a blacksmith on the Hocking estate. So I can start my own shop?"

He asked, still not convinced.

Shawn walked up to him. "Yes, You find a building you want to have. Take all the equipment, and supplies from the shop on Hocking land and start your own business. Barbara will record it and it will be final."

"I want a house in the country with cattle." The big man with the long hair and bushy beard said loudly.

"Then we will ride to Hocking land and you can take ten of his cattle. Only ten that should give you a good start.

"A young man stepped up, "I want to raise sheep and goats. Do I get the same deal?"

"Yes, but only ten of each. Barbara will record each transaction. If someone wants to get greedy and take more, they will deal with the Kingsguard."

Men and women stepped up to Barbara as she recorded the house and business, for each individual. Shawn rode out to the Hocking estate and watched as men began taking cattle, sheep, goats, chickens, and pigs. The men on the estate protested. Shawn spoke with them concerning how the land had been confiscated by the Queen. He believed it would be only fair to share with all the people what the Hocking family had been able to gain for themselves. The men rode to town and also claimed a house or farm for their own.

Two weeks later Traven accompanied a large group of wagons to the village of Dell. Inside the wagons were supplies and people. Many of the women who were working in brothels left heading for the town to start a new life. Young couples with small children arrived also wanting a fresh start. Most of the couples were from large estates and did not want to labor under their current Noble family.

The town was beginning to fill up as business started. Bakery's, inns, potters, tinsmith's, and others were supplied with resources needed.

Land and houses outside the village were occupied by people raising cattle, sheep, goats, pigs and dairies.

A young man with four men rode into the village. He stepped off his horse going to a young man and young woman. He grabbed the man saying loudly, "you are a runaway surf, You will return immediately to my Father's estate."

Traven walked up to the man pushing him aside. "What's the meaning of this?"

The young man squared off as the four men pulled their swords. Shawn walked up beside Traven as both men had their swords out. Barbara standing beside Shawn said in a quiet voice. "Please let's calm down. Now good sir what is the meaning of this?"

The young man sneered at Barbara. "I don't have to answer to a winch. I'm taking these surf's back to my Father's estate."

Barbara put her hand on Shawn's arm. "Calm, please Shawn, Traven, let's be calm." She smiled. "Queen Casandra has decreed that all who want to travel to Dell and settle in this town may do so. That includes any Surf. These people are not slaves. That practice was outlawed many generations ago. They are free people to go as they please."

"Shut your mouth. These Surfs belong on my Father's Estate."

"Okay, then Traven, commander of the Queen's army and my cutie patootie, will end your life." Barbara stepped back.

Shawn snapped his head around. "That nickname is not appropriate for this situation." He looked at Traven. "I'm not sure I can take you in a sword fight, and I really don't want to try. But if you call me that nickname, I'll try. He looked at the other four men who were laughing. All of you are gonna die."

The men stepped back as Traven and Shawn stepped forward.

The young man stepped back as he stared at the two men.

"This is an outrage, you have no right to interfere. I am a Nobleman by birth!"

"Then take it up with the Queen!" Barbara said, raising her voice. "Or die, your choice!"

The young man was red in the face. He turned and walked to his horse and mounted. The four men followed him grinning.

Shawn put his sword in his sheath. "I mean it Traven, call me that silly name and you and I will be exchanging steel."

Traven replaced his sword bowing low and said "yes my lord."

"Smart alec," Shawn said as he took Barbara's hand walking off.

Traven arrived back at the castle a week later with a letter Barbara had written. Also were the transcripts of the men and women who had set up business and farms. Cassie smiled, "I am pleased with the response. I hope with so many of the veterans, who have responded, the robbing of travelers will be reduced. I understand a Priest has been assigned. " She looked up smiling, "I believe it is appropriate for the livestock from the Hocking estate to be divided among the peasants. Was there any trouble?"

Traven told of the young man wanting Surfs returned to an estate. How it had been stopped before violence occurred. Cassie smiled then put her hand to her mouth and laughed. Reben smiled a rare smile, and Micha laughed at the silly nickname Barbara had given Shawn.

Traven said "I believe it broke the tension, and there was no bloodshed."

Cassie turned to Reuben, "You are not to call Shawn that name, I mean it Reuben do not do it. That means you too Micha, no one is to tease Shawn. I believe you are correct Traven, the tension was broken because of Barbara. I am glad there was no bloodshed." She stood up walking to her library laughing.

Simon left the following day. He had stayed and speaking with Cassie was able to have several trade agreements negotiated. He was pleased with the reception but was anxious to return home. Reuben sent six of the Queens Guard to escort him home. He stopped in Dell and was amazed at the transformation. He would arrive home a week later.

Chapter XIX

Micha walked into the library Cassie used as her study. He stopped seeing she was reading. She looked up smiling, "whats going on Micha?"

"Three men from the Island of Wixon want to see you. One of the men is very insistent."

Cassie sat up, "What is his name?"

"Rupert Stalling." Micha said looking at Cassie.

Cassie closed her eyes thinking why him? Why would the King send Rupert who was arrogant, egotistical and always puffed up. She knew him well. He was ten years older than her and had been one of her tutors. She despised him.

"Tell the men I will see them in the morning. Have them shown to a room and made comfortable."

Micha turned and left the room. He returned later saying, "Rupert Stallings says he is to see you now."

"No, tell him I will see him in the morning." Cassie was irritated knowing Rupert was pushing Micha to be seen. He had a high opinion of himself. He would of course dictate when he was seen.

The following morning Cassie had the three men wait until mid morning. Reuben insisted on being present when she was seeing dignitaries. The men from Wixon Island were no threat.

When the three men were escorted in by Micha she could tell Reupert was angry.

He did not bow and immediately began talking. "Cassie, did this young man not inform you I have been waiting to see you? I am the Ambassador of the King of Wixon Island!"

"Micha informed me of your arrival."

Reupert stood glaring at Casie. He took a deep breath and let it out.

"Well the King is pleased with you on the throne and Axel is out. King Hershall extends to you his compliments. Rupert smiling said, "this will be an excellent colony."

Cassie sat up slowly, her anger was burning hot inside her. "A colony for Wixon Island, did I hear you correctly? King Hershall believes this Kingdom will be his colony?"

Reupert smiled smugly, "Well of course. You are a Wixon Princess as was your Mother. You are his niece. I'm sure he will name you regent and allow you to rule under his authority. There are several eligible royal men including myself, who he will no doubt want you to marry."

Cassie stood up, her dark eyes flashing anger. "You expect me to hand over this Kingdom, my Father ruled with my Mother? How dare you walk so boldly and rudely into my throne room, with such disrespect and insult." She turned to Reunen, "I want this man removed from here immediately! Take this ass to the dungeon!"

Reupert was shocked. Reuben approached quickly, grabbing his arm dragging him out. "You, You do not treat the Ambassador of Wixon Island this way!" he screamed in outrage. "I represent the KIng!"

Micha opened the door as Reuben dragged the man out. The other men started to leave. "No, you are not to leave." She looked at the men of her guard. "These men are not to leave."

Two guards immediately walked up and stood by the men. They did not speak as they looked helplessly at the Queen.

Reuben dragged the screaming man down the steps to the dungeon. He opened the door and threw Reupert in. He walked in grabbing the man picking him up, his fingers gripped the smaller man's neck. Reupert standing on his tiptoes, his eyes bulging as he struggled to breathe. He shook Reupert, and in a low voice said "You did not bow, or address the Queen with respect. You insult her with your arrogance."

He released the man slapping him hard. Reupert fell to the ground.

"You will show respect to My Lady or I will remove your head and place it on a pike near the front gate as a warning to all who enter to show respect."

Cassie's fists were clenched in rage as she waited for Reuben to return. "Reuben, you will escort these men out." She looked at the two men who were terrified. "Inform King Hershell I am no reagent, I am Queen." She turned and walked toward her library.

Reuben grabbed both men who walked quickly to the door Micha opened. He walked across the large open space and out of the two large doors. On the patio he threw both men down the steps. He walked down and picked them up pushing them into their carriage. He slapped a horse's rump and watched as the carriage left quickly.

Cassie sat quietly in the dark room for a long while then stood up going outside. She walked out of the back of the castle through the garden and to the field where the men were practicing. She watched Reuben working with men as well as Traven watching men practicing with wooden daggers. She knew she had to settle down. Cassie walked to Traven, "how are the young noblemen doing?"

"They're soft, and don't have the stamina to stay on the field all day. They are learning and I no longer hear about them being of noble birth. I believe it will take time for them to adjust, it will happen." Traven said matter of factly.

Cassie walked to the soldiers barracks and to the back where she saw Paul laying in bed. She smiled as she sat down on his bed. He looked bad. His skin was yellow and his breathing was labored.

Cassie placed her small hand on his face. He smiled at her.

"My Lady, you shouldn't come in here. It's for foul vulgar soldiers."

She smiled "my favorite kind of people. You don't look well my friend."

"I feel a bit ill. I should be up in a few days." He smiled weakly.

"I wish I could heal the scars you carry inside you. I regret you are in so much pain with the burden you have," She whispered.

Paul smiled as a tear ran down his cheek. "I hope the good book is right and the Lord forgives me."

Cassie kissed him on the cheek. "He has and you will be welcome in his Kingdom. He knows you have already been to hell."

Cassie stood up as Paul fell asleep. She walked outside seeing Traven and Reuben with Shawn.

"Did the King's Ambassador find his accommodations acceptable?"

"No, he whined and cried like a small spoiled girl. I explained the proper way to approach a Lady." Reuben said, looking at Cassie.

"Oh, I'm sure you did." She sighed, "Paul is failing, please let me know..." She stopped talking and looked at Traven. He nodded his head.

Two days later Micha walked into Cassie's library. She turned and looked at him.

"I have a mission for you." She reached under the table picking up a leather satchel. She handed it to him. "You will need to pack and prepare to be gone, possibly a week perhaps longer. I am sending you to the Island of Wixon. You will deliver a message." She looked at him seriously, "I will show you the proper etiquette when you meet the King. Also you will need to know how to respond when asked a question. So let's get started."

Chapter XX

Micha leaned against the ship hull watching dolphins swimming ahead of the ship. He grinned seeing such a sight. The young man had never seen anything like the graceful dolphins. He had left the castle with Evan and Wallace escorting him to Seaside. He carried a thick envelope the Queen wanted him to deliver to King Hershell. Manny was in port and said it would be a pleasure to carry the Queens valet to the Island of Wixon. Manny had told Micha he had not seen any pirates for months. But if they were lucky they might find some and he could help chase them off. Micha said he would rather not see pirates.

The trip was pleasant with a fair wind. It was cold in early spring. Micha thought of how things had changed for him. He had traveled across the mountains fighting bandits and wild animals. He had been an orphan boy whose old Aunt thought he was a nuisance, and when she died he lived with Bill who was mean. He remembered how Beth had brought him clothes and blankets. She often brought him food he missed her. Now he was the Queen's valet. He believed the God in heaven he prayed to each evening had brought him to this point in his life.

When the ship docked. Manny found a man with a cart to take Micha to the castle. Micha was nervous. Cassie had told him he would not be harmed. He should remember he was the Queen's messenger and would be treated with respect. He wished Traven, or Shawn had come with him.

The cart pulled by a small donkey walked across the drawbridge, the small hooves echoing off the oak planks, stopping at a large gate that was closed. Micha jumped down and reached into his leather purse taking out four coppers.

The man smiled, shaking his head. "No, my young lord, I'm honored to carry the Queens Valet. May God be with her." The man turned the donkey and left.

Micha walked up to the gate seeing two soldiers. He handed one of them a letter Cassie said was his letter of introduction. The Guard stared at the letter then showed it to the other guard. He walked off with the letter. A short while later a young man walked to the gate holding the letter. He looked at the letter then at Micha.

"Are you Micha Stewart?"

"Yes Sir."

The man looked confused. He instructed the gate to be opened. He motioned for Micha to follow him. They walked up the cobblestone road leading to the castle. Micha was in awe seeing the magnificent castle. It was massive and the stone work was beautiful.

Micha followed the young man into the castle. He slowed down to look at the beautiful carved doors. The carvings were of men hunting wild bears, tigers and other wild animals. Men and women in gardens and meadows were carved in the door.

He stopped as the man holding the letter spoke in low tones to an older man. The man looked at Micha and frowned. He walked to him and asked in a gruff voice.

"You are the messanger for Queen Casandra?"

"Yes Sir, She has given me a letter to deliver to King Hershell."

"Give it to me I will deliver it. You will wait here and I will return with his answer."

"No." Micha said standing as tall as he could. Queen Casandra's order was to deliver it directly to King Hershell."

The older man with thining white hair scowled down at Micha.

"The King does not have time to hear from children. I will deliver the letter, boy."

Micha shook his head. "I am to deliver the letter."

"Then it won't be delivered, boy." The man said angrily.

"Ok, I guess you decide who the King sees or not." Micha said quietly. He walked to a chair and sat down.

The older man stood staring at Micha, he turned abruptly walking to a door going inside, shutting it behind him. A man walked up to Micha looking at him. He was tall and dark. His head was bald and his face clean shaven. He smiled, saying "That looks like a Rangers dagger."

"It is." Micha said looking at the man as he continued to sit. The man was tall with a large barrel chest and stout arms.

"Where did you get a Ranger's dagger?"

"A Ranger gave it to me. Reuben, who is Queen Casandra's Captain of her Highness guards, gave it to me."

The door opened and the older man with white hair walked out frowning.

"King Hershell has agreed to see you young man. Follow me."

Micha stood up as the tall man said "you are not allowed to have a weapon in the throne room."

Micha united the dagger and handed it to the Man. He looked at it and nodded his head at Micha.

The man led Micha into the throne room. Micha had been told it would be full of people. He stopped in front of the throne. He saw a man of medium size who was dark with dark eyes looking at him. He had a crown on his head. An attractive dark woman with dark eyes and black hair with a crown on her head watched him.

The Man in a loud Voice said "Your Highness, Micha Stewart Valet and Messenger from Queen Casandra."

Micha bowed low then turned and bowed to the Queen. He reached into his large leather satchel removing the letter.

"A letter to your Highness from Queen Casandra."

He handed the large envelope to the man who walked forward and handed the King the sealed envelope.

King Hershell looked at the envelope but did not open it. He stared down at Micha.

"I understand Queen Casandra placed my Ambasador in the dungeon and treated my emissaries with disrespect. Is it true?"

"Yes." Mica said, trying to speak up.

"Why would Queen Casandra do such a disreputable thing to a visiting Ambasador?"

"He disrespected her. Your Ambasador did not bow showing respect. He referred to her intimately using her nickname; only a few have been extended that privilege." Micha spoke low. He was nervous.

"Lock him up, or hang the impudent fool!" a woman's voice screamed across the room. The King looked at the woman then to his wife. Anger on his face was apparent.

"That woman has no right to lock up my son!" She screamed louder.

Queen Asha turned to look at a tall woman in uniform. The woman immediately walked to the woman saying in a low firm voice. "You have not been recognized by the King Lady Ada. Speak out again and I will have no choice but to remove you."

The Ladies face was in a rage. "Remove me, I am the Queen's Aunt! My son is the King's ambassador and he has been mistreated by this half-breed Queen!"

The woman in uniform reached out, taking the woman's arm and escorted her out. The woman in uniform walked back standing beside the Queen.

The King was obviously upset. "Perhaps I should return the compliment Queen Casandra has paid me and lock up her messenger."

Micha stood quiet showing little emotion.

"What do you think Queen Casandra would do If the King locked you up young Man?" Queen Asha asked in a soft voice.

"She would send Reuben, Traven, and Shawn to get me out. Paul would want to come but he is too sick." Micha said looking at the beautiful Queen.

"Three men? Queen Casandra would send three men to rescue you?" The King said, leaning forward looking directly at Micha.

"Yes." Micha said just above a whisper.

The King sat back. The woman in uniform stepped forward "with your permission my Lord."

The King nodded. The woman walked up to Micha looking down at him. Micha looked up at her, she was tall and an attractive woman.

"There are twenty four soldiers in the King's guard in his throne room. Twelve men and twelve women. I know Queen Casandra and I know she is well aware of this since she served in the Queensguard. "Do you believe three men can defeat the Kingsguard?"

"Yes," Micha said quietly. They followed my lady into King Axel's throne room and took it without bloodshed. Reuben is a Royal Ranger, Traven, and Shawn served in the war as did Paul."

The woman stood silently looking down at Micha. "Impossible the Royal Rangers were all killed. I was there. Casandra tried to save one but he was beyond help." She said surprised.

"May I approach," the tall man who had taken Micha's dagger asked.

"You may," the King said, now intrigued.

The man walked up to the woman and handed her the dagger. "The young man had this on prior to entering. He said a Royal Ranger gave it to him."

The woman reached out, taking the dagger. She removed it, inspecting it carefully. She replaced it in the sheath and handed it back to the man. She looked at the Queen

"I believe it is a Royal Ranger's dagger." She looked back at Micha. "So he lived, the Ranger who Casandra was told was beyond help?"

"Yes." Micha said quietly.

The woman walked to a large man standing close to the King. He was the Captain of the Kingsguard and Queensguard.

"A Royal Ranger, two battle hardened veterans, I would give them a thirty-five percent chance."

"Closer to fifty percent chance." he said looking at her.

The woman bowed to the King and Queen and walked back to her place beside the Queen.

"How did Casandra take the throne with four men, when the Kingsguard were on duty?" The King asked, leaning forward.

"She paid the guards. They had not been paid for months. Shawn went to the Treasury and paid them all their back pay including a bonus. I don't believe the Kingsguard liked the King. They are loyal to Queen Casandra." Micha said, speaking louder."

The King looked at the Man beside him. "Fifty percent chance three men kill my guard?"

"Yes." He said, turning and looking at the King. "I recognize the name Traven, I believe he is Tisdale, we were at the crossings where Chamberlain was making his stand to prevent King Axel's men from flanking King Jarrod. Those men were fighting to the last man. Shawn, I'm not sure about, but I have no doubt he will be a formidable foe. Reuben Byne was Commander of the Royal Rangers. I was there with Tory, and Casandra. The head healer Wilma Scott told Casandra he was too far gone. She stayed since she had been wounded to help him, If he did survive. It will be a fierce battle. They are to be respected, Sire."

The King sat quietly looking at the letter. "Have this young gentleman taken to a room so he can rest."

The woman beside the Queen stepped out saying "follow me."

Micha was taken up a flight of stairs to a small room. The woman smiled as she walked in. "I am Tory Allan, Cassie was my friend. We served together in the Queensguard and war." Tory laughed as she sat down. "She is smart, and I believe no one should underestimate her. Please tell me how she is doing?"

Micha had been warned to be careful of saying too much. So he guarded his words as he told of the journey across the mountains. How Cassie had been recognized by the Bishop. Reuben, Traven, Shawn and Paul who were his friends. When he finished Tory patted him on his back and left.

Chapter XXI

When the King stood up everyone in the room bowed. He glanced at the Queen who followed him. They both walked into a small room which served as his study. The Queen said "I am sorry Hershell, Ada was out of line."

He turned to look at her. "Lady Ada will never be allowed in my throne room."

"I understand, and I will speak to her." The Queen whispered.

The King walked up to her. "I was against sending Reupert as an Ambassador. He has insulted Casandra with his arrogance. You convinced me because your Aunt believes she is important because of her Royal connections."

"I am truly sorry, Herschell. I was wrong. It will not happen again." She whispered.

He walked to a table and sat down. The Queen continued to stand. The King began reading the letter. After a long while he sat the letter down and shook his head

"I cannot believe this. That fool Reupert said Casandra would be a regent since I would turn her kingdom into a colony."

The Queen put her hand to her mouth in shock. "He didn't."

"Not only that He told her She would be marrying a Royal. Which insinuates a man will move in and run her kingdom for her. She is prepared to fight the Wixon army. She does not have an army that can stand against ours, but she will lead them."

The King was furious. The Queen said "I don't believe we should go to war."

"No, King Jarrod would fight with her and the other smaller Kingdoms would also. This is ridiculous."

He walked to the door opening it saying to the older man at the back of the room. "Have Dylan join me and the Queen."

Dylan the second son of King Hearshell and Queen Asha walked in and sat down. The King handed him the letter. Dylan looked at the King when he finished reading the letter from Queen Casandra.

"You will go to Queen Casandra and speak to her. Tell her that Reupert is an Idiot, who spoke out of turn. I am not looking for any colonies and she does not have to worry about that. Speak to her about an alliance. You need not make this right. Bring that Ass Repurt home so I can hang him.

"Okay. I'll do my best to clean this mess up." Dylan said looking at his angry Father.

"You are not going to hang Reupert. He is of Royal blood. Ada is my mothers sister." Queen Asha said shocked looking at her husband.

"Royal blood or not He will hang." The King said definitely.

"No, you will not hang Repuert. I realize he is a fool and I never should have insisted you send him." She said, lowering her voice.

"I'll hang him, and you." The King said, leaning back in his chair.

"You are not going to hang me, your wife, and Queen."

I'll hang Dylan also." The King said, looking at his son.

"I haven't done anything? Why hang me?"

"When I hang your mother you will fight and try to save her. That is rebellion against the Crown." So you will have to hang."

"Stop being ridiculous Hershell. You are not going to hang anyone. I know you're upset. Take a day to think about it." Queen Asha said as she walked out of the room.

The King stood up and walked out with Dylan.

"You wouldn't really hang your favorite son would you father?"

"I wouldn't enjoy it if that makes you feel better." KIng Hershell said with a slight smile on his face.

The following day Dylan spoke with several advisors concerning how he should approach Queen Casandra. He remembered her. She was smart and deadly with a sword, dagger including the bow and arrows. Many of his classmates did not accept her since she was half Wixon. He had always admired her. The King, who was Dylan's Grandfather had agreed to have his daughter marry King Benjamin for a political alliance. He remembered how beautiful Casandra was. They had fought in the war and she was a fierce warrior. She was the finest archer and swordsman the Army had. The commanders often would speak with her prior to a battle. She was smart and often her suggestions on pending battles helped.

He and Micha boarded the ship together five days later. Manny set sail and headed for Seaside.

Micha walked into the library bowing low. Cassie smiled "welcome home Micha. Tell me how was you're trip?"

"It was good. I delivered your message and like you said the King was not too happy. He asked why I shouldn't be locked up. I told him Reuben, Traven and Shawn would come for me. A lady yelled I should be locked up. A guard took her out. I saw the town and countryside. The Island is beautiful with farms and businesses. The army was training. They have a lot of men and women in their army."

Cassie smiled. I'm glad you enjoyed Wixon Island. "I understand you were accompanied by a guest."

"Dylan Kelly the King and Queen's second son. He's a nice guy. He wants to speak with you."

"Make sure he is comfortable. I will see him in two days." She hesitated, and reached out taking both hands of Micha, "I'm sorry Micha to have to tell you that Paul died after you left. He was given a soldier's burial with full honors."

Micha felt the lump in his throat. He and Paul had been friends. Paul had taught him how to shoot the bow. He would miss him. "He was sick for a long time." Micha said just above a whisper. Micha went to his room.

The following day Micha went to the Market with Dylan. The people talked with him knowing he was Wixon. They found him fascinating and he enjoyed talking with the people. Although they were former enemies. Most had accepted the war was the result of King Axel and most were willing to move on.

Micha and Dylan rode out of the town of Kichita to see the country. He was able to see how the people of the war torn country were rebuilding. Micha told him of how the Village of Dell was being rebuilt with war veterans, and other settlers. Dylan was impressed.

Dylan bowed low and smiled seeing Cassie. "I extend my Father's sincere apology for the rudeness of his Ambassador Queen Casandra. I hope you will forgive the King for his lapse of judgment with his choice of people to speak for him."

"I accept the King's apology, I know Rupert well and know he can be puffed up at times."

Dyan smiled, "Thank you Cas., he caught himself. Queen Casandra."

Cassie smiled.

Dylan handed Micha a sealed envelope. "A letter to you from the King. He would like to have an alliance and trade agreements."

"I look forward to our nations becoming close."

Cassie told Dylan word had come that the Pope would be in Kachita in the early summer months. Dylan said the King and Queen would be honored to be at her coronation.

The meeting was cordial. Dylan asked if Reupert could be released from the dungeon. He did not plan on leaving immediately since there was more he wanted to discuss with the Queen. Cassie agreed he should be released. She smiled, saying, "Traven, would you bring the rude man from Wixon Island here."

Traven walked into the cell grabbing Reupert pulling him to his feet.

"You have an audience with the Queen, you royal turd."

"I won't be talked to that way by a commoner. I have Royal Wixon blood." Reupert stammered.

Traven threw the door open from the dungeon, dragging the protesting Reupert up the stairs and across the large open room. He dragged the complaining man out onto the large patio saying, "You may have Royal blood but you smell like the back end of a mule with bad gas. I'm not taking you to Queen Casandra with your stench."

Traven walked to the edge of the patio throwing Reupert into a large horse trough. He jumped down and held Repurt's head down then pulled it up. Reupert gasped for air as Traven pushed him back down into the water.

Reupert was pulled out of the horse trough roughly and dragged up the steps and across the open room. He was pushed roughly into the throne room dripping wet.

Queen Casandra looked at Reupert surprised. She looked at Traven.

"He needed a bath before seeing you, my lady."

"I was thrown into a horse trough by this thug! I demand he be locked up! I will not be treated this way!" Reupert howled in protest."

Dylan looked at Traven. Then looked at Reupert putting his hand on his wet shoulder.

"With your permission I will take my leave, Queen Casandra."

"Of course. She said, trying not to laugh. "Micha ask Lou Ann to take Dylan and Reupert to a room. Also have a bathtub brought in so Rupert may bathe.

Dylan and Reupert sat quietly the following morning as the Noblemen Lester Hocking was brought into the throne room. They were surprised a trial was being held for a Nobleman. Kingdoms always held any indiscretion by a Noble in private.

Lester Hocking was outraged as he was brought to a trial. He demanded to be released along with his wife due to being a Nobleman. Cassie only looked at him passively then turned to Thomas Sands, her head treasurer. The amount of taxes due was given to each Noble in the room. Also were funds that he kept given by King Jarrod. The amount of taxes he received from Surfs, but not given to the crown treasury.

He stood defiantly staring at Casandra. "How do you answer not giving money to peasants who were suffering as you lived a luxury lifestyle." Cassie asked from her throne.

"I owe you no explanation. You are not my Queen." He sneered."

She looked at the Noblemen who sat silently. "All of you have paid what is due to the crown. Yet Mr. Hocking refuses to pay. I am recognized by the Bishop and the Pope will crown me Queen. Is there a reason I should not hang this man?"

"Hang me? You have no authority, Witch!" Lester screamed. He walked toward the throne. Reuben stepped forward as Lester stopped, seeing the big man walk toward him. Reuben pushed Lester hard as the man fell backwards. Reuben walked back standing by Cassie.

"I asked a question." She stood up, obviously angry. In a controlled angry voice asked, "Noblemen have not hesitated to hang a surf for violating a law. Keeping the others in line I believe is the common belief. Well are you going to sit there in all your arrogance and convince me this man who has done worse should not be hanged!"

Harold said quietly. "He is of Noble blood, it has been tradition to allow more leniency."

"So he should not be hanged? Do you want me to pardon him because he is a Nobleman? Be careful how you answer Gentlemen." Cassie had turned and looked directly at the men. None of them spoke.

"This man is banished. Reuben, please see this man and his wife are removed from my castle and make sure they cross the borders to any kingdom. Should they return they will be hanged. I will give leniency for the sake of tradition for Noblemen, although I believe it is a poor practice."

Reuben looked at two men in the Queensguard. "As the Queen has commanded, see her orders are followed."

Two guards stepped forward picking up Lester taking him out of the room. Cassie stood up looking at the men. "I have told you gentlemen change is coming. You will stand with me or against me. You chose."

Dylan stayed at the castle for another week. He observed the army and their training. He spoke with many of the Noblemen who complained of their treatment. He was not sympathetic to them. They had been loyal to Axel.

Micha escorted Dylan into the throne room early in the morning. Dylan told Reupert to stay outside. He of course protested, but Dylan did not want him to be in the presence of Cassie.

He bowed to Cassie and said, "I will take my leave and will deliver your letter to my father. I look forward to our countries being allies."

Cassie nodded then watched as Dylan walked up to Reuban.

"The King was pleased to hear that one of his Royal Rangers survived. He is recalling you to Wixon Island. His desire is for you to rebuild his Royal Rangers forces. You will be in charge of training them."

Cassie stood up. "Reuben is Captain of my guard. He will remain in my Kingdom and serve me."

Dylan was surprised. "The Royal Rangers were started by my Grandfather, their mission is to Wixon Island. You do not decide for King Hershell or defy his order."

"He was my Grandfather as well. Do not instruct me on the mission of Royal Rangers. I am well aware of their mission. Royal Rangers are to protect the crown of Wixon. My Mother was a Princess of Wixon Island, as am I. Reuben is fulfilling that mission. Protecting the crown of Wixon." Cassie's small hands were clenched as her eyes blazed with fury.

"He has been recalled by the King who he serves. I will be taking this Ranger back to Wixon Island as has been ordered." Dylan said, raising his voice.

"No, you will not. Where was King Hershell's order when Axel attacked this Kingdom? Where my Mother and two Brothers died in this throne room defending the Kingdom. His Sister and nephews died. He refused to allow me to come and fight with them. He finally acted when Sistra was attacked, who was an ally. One year later he sent the Royal Rangers. Not the Wixon Army. Rangers who were recruited from other lands to serve him. They of course are not Wixon by birth, so it is easier to sacrifice them and not those born on the Island. No, I will defy this order from my Uncle who hesitated. Reuben is serving a Wixon Queen."

Dylan was angry and tried to control his emotions. He had not expected this defiance from Cassie.

"The King was in negotiations with King Axel and other realms trying to find a peaceful solution to the war. You will not sit in judgment of my Father. I served as did many of our people, and too many died."

"I am not judging him or the other realms who were slow to respond. I was at the meadows where the Royal Rangers fought to the last man. Wilma Scott the head healer of our unit said Rueben was too far gone to waste our time on. She abandoned him as did the Wixon army to die. I stayed with him and by God's grace he survived. He will stay with me."

"Are you willing to die for that stance?" Dylan said with a sneer.

Cassie walked to the guards who were posted along the wall.

"Stand at attention" she said to them. She reached down, removing a sword from Dalton and turning threw it to Dylan who caught it. She removed the sword from Ethan and said as she walked toward Dylan.

"Reuben, you will remain in the throne room and no harm will befall Prince Dylan should he return." She stopped at the back door. "You and I, Dylan, will settle this dispute outside."

Dylan stood shocked. He dropped the sword. "I will not fight with Royal Blood my cousin." He walked out of the room.

Cassie walked to the sword and picked it up. She walked to the guards and handed both swords back. She turned and walked to Reuben. She stopped in front of him. With emotion in her voice speaking just above a whisper said,

"I give you leave Reuben to go or stay."

"I will remain."

She walked out of the room to her Library. Reuben followed her. She stood in the middle of the room trying to gain control of her emotions. Cassie turned looking at Reuben. "You are my friend and closest advisor, and I would trade my life for yours in an instant. I love you Reuben."

"I am your guardian, protector, advisor and friend. I will give my life for you freely. If the King demands I return and you are threatened in any way, I will fall on my sword."

"I know," she said softly as a tear ran down her cheek.

Chapter XXII

Barbara walked up the steps sitting in a chair next to Shawn. The rain had just started falling, "nice to have rain," She said smiling. "It will give us a break from the heat. I love summer rains."

"I agree." Shawn sat quietly for a while then said "there's a new Priest in the village."

"I know he's repairing the old chapel. He's a nice young man."

"We should go pay him a visit. Have him marry us." Shawn was looking directly at Barbara.

She turned to look at him. "You haven't asked me."

"Marry me Barbara." He said smiling.

"Sounds more like a demand."

"Will you marry me, my lady?" He ask, smiling broadly.

She sat quietly for some time looking at him. "No secrets, I want you to know everything about me."

"I know enough, whatever is in the past can stay there. I want to marry you."

Barbara looked down, shaking her head. "No, you should know everything. I hate surprises, and secrets I've never known one to be kept." She sat quietly looking down as a tear ran down her cheek. She wiped it away and looked at Shawn.

"I grew up in the castle. My Father was the Chief Clerk. I helped him with his duties. I knew the royal family. I remember Cassandra, she was a strong willed girl. Not bad but she could be stubborn. Her older brother Michale was ten years older than her. We became close. I had his child. I never told anyone who the Father was. Of course the gossips in the castle were aware of the fact Michael and I spent a lot of time together.

When the castle fell, after King Benjamin died. Michael was killed along with his older brother and Mother. They never surrendered, all of them fought to their deaths

"Barbara sat quietly as she looked away watching the rain fall.

"I was taken when King Axel's men entered the castle." She whispered. "I fought them but they beat me, and…" Barbara began crying.

Shawn stood up taking her hand pulling her up. He hugged her as she cried.

"It was wrong," He whispered to her."

Barbara leaned against Shawn. "King Axel began searching for all the records of any relatives of King Benjamin. He ordered Casandra killed. I was scared He would find out Michael was King Benjamin's grandson. I knew many people were fleeing the country. I gave Michael to a family who were going across the mountains. I had an elderly Aunt who lived at the foot of the Mountains at Solace." Barbara began to cry "I never saw him again."

"Okay, so will you marry a soldier who is not perfect?" Shawn asked.

"Yes, but you have to come to church with me." She said, stepping back.

"I don't go to church. If you want to, that's fine." He said lowering his voice.

Why, and tell the truth." She said looking into his eyes.

"Me and the Lord's not on speaking terms."

"Because of the war and the horror you have seen. "

"Yes. He could have stopped it." Shawn said, growing angry.

"He didn't start the war, King Axel did. He is a mean spirited man who is filled with pride and lust for power. The Lord would have to withdraw the gift of free will to mankind if he chose to stop the war which was started by a man. Then you would just do as he commands instead of what you decide. The choices mankind decides would have been taken away. You will go to church with me, cutie patootie."

"You're going to stop calling me that stupid nickname." He said frowning.

"No, you're my cutie patootie. And you will go to church with me after I marry you."

They were married the following afternoon. Shawn often laying in bed late at night next to Barbara thought of the young boy who was Barbara's son. He had a thought that was in his mind. He wondered if it could be true.

Greg Abbot was standing on the pier watching his ship being unloaded. His company was doing great since the pirates were no longer raiding him or other ships. Traven had allowed him to use the pirates' ships for his business. Twenty percent of all profits would go to Queen Casandra. He watched a large ship dock on the pier next to his ship. People began walking down the gangplank. He saw a young pretty woman with black hair carrying a leather bag make her way down the gangplank. She stopped on the pier and looked around. She scanned the area looking at the crowd.

Greg approached the young woman. "Excuse me my lady, is your name Beth?"

"She smiled a bright smile looking up at the tall man as she blushed. She had not been called a lady before. That title was only for the Nobles.

"Yes" she said just above a whisper. My name is Beth O'Bannon."

Greg's smile grew larger as he reached out taking the leather bag. He looked at the other men who were watching him. "You are Traven's friend from Solace!"

"Yes I am. Is Traven here?"

"No, my lady, he is at the castle." He looked at the other men on the pier and roared,

"This is Beth O'Bannon, Travens friend!"

The men gathered around her shaking her hand. Some of the men hugged her. They all followed her down the pier as Greg held her hand.

When they stepped off the pier, women who were working stopped and came to greet her. She was surprised as they all wanted to meet her. One young woman said

"You must be tired Beth, you can stay at the inn and rest. I'm sure we can find an escort to take you to the castle."

Beth was overwhelmed. "Yes, that would be great. I am anxious to see Traven. How is he? I hope he has not been in any trouble. I know he can be impulsive sometimes."

The men and women laughed. The woman said smiling, "He is not in trouble, but he did help drive the pirates away from our shores, which we are grateful for."

The trip to Kachita was pleasant. Greg had arranged for a carriage to take Beth to the capitol. The older man who had spent his life on the sea told Beth of what he knew of the kingdom. They stopped at a small inn as it grew dark. The people were gracious. She arrived in Kachita early in the following afternoon.

Beth walked up the stairs seeing a man in uniform standing next to the large door. She stopped and said nervously. "May I enter? "I believe my friend Traven is here."

The young man's eyes went wide. "Yes of course." He said as he opened the door. She was nervous never seeing such a large city and the castle was inspiring. Walking into the castle she was in awe. The large open room was something she had never seen before. She smiled when she saw Micha sitting in a chair. He looked at her then with recognition in his eyes he jumped up running to her. Beth hugged him tightly then stepped back looking at him.

"You have grown Micha, and you are so finely dressed. You are a young handsome gentleman."

Micha grinned. "I'm the Queen's valet." He grasped her hand "I will announce you to the Queen."

"Oh no, Micha you must not. I cannot see the Queen!" Beth said horrified.

Micha smiled. "I will go find Traven." He looked at a young guard, Evan who was standing by the door. "This is Beth, she is Traven's friend."

Evan smiled and bowed, "It is a pleasure to meet you my lady."

Micha opened the door and went inside. He went to the library where Cassie was inside. He opened the door and stepped inside. Reuben and Cassie were talking. They both looked at him. He grinned at Reuben. "Beth has arrived." He looked at Cassie, "with your permission may I have leave to bring Traven here?"

"Well of course Micha, Have Beth come here to wait. There is no reason to have her stay in the lobby." Cassie said smiling.

Beth was hesitant as she followed Micha into the throne room. Micha opened the door to the library as Beth stepped in. she bowed low seeing Cassie.

Cassie stood up, going to her and hugging her. It is a pleasure to see you Beth. How was your trip?"

"Fine my lady, I was sick on the ship because of the constant rocking, but it was good to be on dry land." Beth stammered.

She saw Reuben stand up. He was the biggest man she had ever seen. He looked directly at her. "Would you like me to get you some tea?"

Beth was shocked and surprised that a Royal Ranger who was a battle hardened warrior would offer to get her tea. She was not sure what to say.

"No," thank you" she whispered.

Micha found Traven on the practice field. He ran up to him saying,

"Traven, Beth has arrived. She is in CC's library."

Traven immediately began walking quickly to the castle.

Traven stopped and allowed Micha to enter the library first. He followed him inside seeing Beth stand up. He went to her and hugged her.

Cassie said, "Commander, you have been working hard lately. I believe it would be good to take some time off."

"Thank you," he said smiling."

Reuben stood up. "I'm glad you are here Beth. Now I won't have to hold Traven's hand as he cries himself to sleep every night."

"He's making that up Beth. don't pay any attention to his smart talk." He looked directly in her eyes. "It wasn't every night."

Beth giggled. As She followed Traven out of the room.

King Hershell sat in the dimly lit study staring at the wall. He was angry. Dylan returned with a letter from Cassie. It was more than he had expected and was pleased with the alliance and trade deals. What bothered him was her defiance of his order. He knew she had always been a stubborn child. Her refusal of not allowing the Royal Ranger to return was disappointing. He was furious, he did not like the fact his order had been defied. He also knew she was angry about losing her Mother and two Brothers after her Father had mysteriously died. He as did everyone else believed King Benjamin had been poisoned. He could not let this defiance stand.

He turned as his wife walked in and sat down. She spoke softly,

"I know you are upset Hershell, Cassie has defied your order. Please consider all options. I will not give you advice or attempt to influence you. She did save him and he is loyal to her. You are a devout Christian, what does your heart tell you?"

"I will not be defied. I will discuss this with her at her coronation." He said firmly.

Chapter XIII

Shawn stopped the small carriage in front of the castle steps. He jumped off and walked around the carriage taking Barbara's hand. She stepped down, he leaned over and kissed her lightly on the lips.

He removed the large trunk with their clothes inside. A groomsman led the horse and carriage away.

Shawn sat the trunk down as Micha walked up to them quickly.

"Welcome home Shawn and Barbara. Good to have you here?" he said excitedly.

Barbara smiled and leaned down kissing Micha on the cheek.

"You've grown Micha. You are becoming quite the man."

"Thank you," He said beaming. "Beth is here. She arrived three weeks ago."

Shawn smiled. "I'm glad to hear that maybe she can keep Traven out of trouble."

"Maybe," Mica said grinning. "I will let CC know you are here."

"I'll take the trunk to your room. It is ok if your husband stays in your room isn't it?" Shawn asked, looking serious.

"Yes, cutie you may share my bed."

Shawn walked off as Barbara followed Micha into the throne room to the library.

Barbara sat down and removed a large stack of parchment paper from her leather bag.

"I have all the paperwork of those who are residing in Dell, my lady."

Cassie smiled, "good I'm anxious to see how it is going."

Shawn walked up to Micha and sat down. He looked at the young man and said,

"You have come far Micha since we have left Solace. You have done well."

Micha looked at Shawn, "I believe we all have "you and Traven married, and have the Queens trust." he looked down saying softly, "I wish Paul was here."

Shawn patted him on the back. "I do too, he was a true friend."

They sat quiet for a time when Shawn asked. "Mica why did you live with that man Bill Doughan? Was he a relative?"

"No, I lived with my Aunt Clara Stewart, who was older. She was a seamstress. She died of consumption, when I was seven. I didn't have anywhere else to go so I lived with Bill, " Micha said speaking plainly.

"Did she tell you of your parents? I don't mean to be nosey my friend, I'm just curious."

Micha said "no, she never said who my parents were."

Shawn went to the practice field to speak with Traven and Reuben. He was pleased the men were doing very well in learning the art of warfare. Traven had him work with men using swords.

Later that afternoon Shawn went back to Barbara's room in the castle. She had supper prepared for him when he arrived. He washed up then sat down. Barbara talked of how the Queen was pleased to have so many of the veterans, as well as others settling in Dell. She noticed he was quiet throughout the meal.

"Why are you so quiet, Shawn? Is there anything wrong."

He reached out, taking her hand, helping her stand up as he rose. They walked to a small couch sitting down.

"What was the name of your old Aunt who lived in Solace you sent your son to live with?" He asked as he held her hand.

Barbara was surprised by the question. "Clara Stewart." She said, speaking just above a whisper.

Shawn took a deep breath and allowed it to escape slowly, "Micha is your son. He lived in Solace with his elderly Aunt Clara Stewart. She died of consumption when he was seven. He lived with a man named Bill Doughan who ran the Livery stable. He was not a kind man."

Barbara put her hand to her mouth as she stood up, tears running down her cheeks. Shawn went to her holding her as she cried. After a while she sat down wiping her eyes.

"He does look like Michael. I thought there was something about the young man when I first saw him. Now I see the resemblance. I, I don't know…"

She stopped talking and looked down. "I should tell the Queen, he is her nephew."

"I agree." Shawn said, holding her hand.

The following day Barbara and Shawn walked up to Micha. Barbara stared at him. She said softly, "I need to see the Queen Micha."

Micha stood up walking toward the door. Barbara followed him to the library. He stepped inside saying. "Barbara, your Chief Clerk needs to speak to you my lady."

Cassie was looking at papers, She nodded her head as she continued to read.

Barbara walked in sitting down. Cassie looked up from her papers.

Barbara was quiet as Cassie watched her. She took a deep breath saying "I grew up in the castle as you know. I was close to your older brother, Michael. I had his child. I never revealed who the Father was. King Axel was attempting to rid the kingdom of any Heirs. He put out a bounty on you. Any man that killed you would be paid twenty pieces of silver. I sent my son to live with an Aunt in Solace across the mountains. The same mountains you crossed. Shawn has discovered Micha is my son."

Cassie sat back closing her eyes. She had loved Michael. He had always treated her well. He had spent time with her and had always been kind. She remembered Barbara as a young girl. She asked,"Are you certain?"

"Yes, he resembles Michael, and it was fifteen almost sixteen years ago. Not a day has gone by that I have not thought of him. I named him Michael. I suppose my Aunt called him Micha, and gave him her last name. She was my mothers Aunt."

"We will tell him together." Cassie said, reaching out, taking Barbara's hand.

Micha and Shawn sat in the large lobby area talking when they saw a man in expensive clothes with five men walk in. The man walked up to Micha and sneered at him.

"Boy, go tell the Queen Sydney Davis is here. I need to see her immediately."

Shawn stood up looking at the man, "You should show more respect when you address the Queens Valet."

The Man Laughed, "respect, to a guttersnipe?" He looked at Micha. "I told you to tell the Queen I want to see her now, boy!"

Shawn pulled his sword, "You will show this young man respect or you will be leaving her feet first. You donkey's ass."

The man stepped back as the five men stepped forward with swords drawn. "Do you know who you are speaking to?"

"Yes, a donkey's ass who is about to bloody the Queen's floor."

Evan who was on duty stepped forward as Dalton who was on the outside door also stepped inside. Micha had removed his Dagger. The men looked around, seeing the odds were now close to even.

Shawn said, "now gentlemen let's all calm down. We can work this out as gentlemen." He looked at Sydney, "apologize to this young man or I will kill you."

The door opened as Barbara stepped out. She frowned. "I leave you alone for a few minutes Shawn and bloodshed is about to be spilled on the Queen's beautiful tile floor."

"Yeah I know, but this Noble gentleman was rude to Micha. He will apologize or he and his men are going to die."

Barbara looked at the arrogant Sydney, "He was rude to Micha? Okay, then he should die." she said glaring at Sydney.

"There is no need for this violence." Sydney said now nervous. "I withdraw my remarks."

Shawn stepped past the five men placing the point of his sword under the nobleman's chin. "Not an apology."

"I apologize for my remark," he said through clenched teeth.

Shawn stepped back replacing his sword.

"Okay Micha you should announce this gentleman to the Queen."

Micha replaced his dagger and walked to the door as Ethan and Dalton stepped back. Sydney was escorted into the throne room as he held a handkerchief to his chin that was bleeding.

LATER THAT EVENING Micha knocked on the Queen's door. He had never been to her bedroom. It was opened by Cassie. She smiled down at him. "Come in Micha."

He stepped in seeing Barbara sitting on a settee. Cassie took his hand and walked to a chair where she sat down. She took a breath and smiled at him looking at him in his eyes. "Barbara has something important to tell you."

Tears began running down her cheeks. She wiped them away and said

"Micha you are my son."

Micha was stunned. "Your Father is Michael Conrad, who was the King's son. I sent you to live with my Aunt Clara Stewart when King Axel stormed the castle. I was afraid he would kill you." Barbara put her head down and cried.

Cassie reached out, taking his hand, "you are my nephew."

Micha walked to Barbara putting his arms around her. She put her arms around his neck sobbing. "I'm sorry Micha. I'm so sorry."

Chapter XIV

Micha walked into the throne room and to the library early in the morning. He stepped inside seeing Barbara, Reuben and Traven inside. Cassie turned looking at Micha. She frowned seeing the black eye and swollen nose.

"I don't like seeing my valet with bruises on his face." She turned to look at Reuben. You're being hard on this young man."

"He is being trained as a Royal Ranger. Practice as you will fight and you will fight as you practice. That is the motto of a Ranger." Reuben said flatly.

Cassie drew a deep breath as she looked at Reuben. She knew training was often harsh. She had experienced it herself while training with the Wixon army and Kings guard. Cassie was obviously upset. She looked at Micha "What's going on Micha?"

Micha was quiet as he watched the exchange. He could feel tension in the air. "Prince Jameson McClain from Sistra requests an audience, my Lady." He said softly.

"Please show him in Micha."

Micha walked into the throne room with a man following him. He was young and handsome. He was not tall but he had an athletic build. His hair was brownish red, clean shaven, green eyes with a nice looking face. He was not dressed in expensive clothes.

Jammeson bowed low. He had heard Queen Cassandra was beautiful, but he could not immagin how beautiful she truly was.

"I, I bid you welcome Queen Casandra. My Father King James of Sistra extends his congratulations and his apologies for not being here. He is ailing, and could not make the trip."

Cassie's brow wrinkled, "I am saddened to hear King James is not feeling well. I welcome you Prince Jameson."

Jameson smiled as he handed Micha a sealed envelope. "My Father sends you correspondence. He asks for an alliance with you and your kingdom since the war is over and the evil that was once in the castle has been evicted."

Cassie smiled, "I would welcome an alliance with Sistra."

"Queen Casandra, we ask if an alliance is agreed upon, would it be possible to have our wine merchants cross your roads so we could reach Seaside and hire a ship to take our wine to other countries. The vineyards in Sistra are doing exceptionally well. The former ruler denied access to our wine across his roads. We have a large quantity of wine in warehouses, and seek markets for them. "

Cassie watched the handsome young man closely. He was younger than her, perhaps four or five years. He spoke plainly and was not trying to impress her.

"I believe it would be good to consider this as well as other proposals that will benefit our two countries." She looked down at the letter then looked up. "I would like you to stay in the castle as my guest. We will speak later, and would like you to join me for supper."

Jameson bowed, "I look forward to meeting with you. I accept your gracious invitation to dine with you."

Cassie smiled at Micha, "please accompany Prince Jameson so he may pick up his belongings. Ask Lou Ann to prepare a room so he may be comfortable."

Micha bowed, turned and walked out as Jameson followed him.

Cassie, Traven, Barbara and Reuben sat in the library. Cassie read the letter. When she finished she handed it to Barbara. "What are your thoughts on an alliance with Sistra?"

Barbara sat the letter down after reading it. "King Benjamin and King James had an alliance for years. Trade was established between each country, and both did well. I would say it is a great opportunity for us both."

Reuben and Traven agreed.

"What are your impressions of Prince Jameson?" Cassie asked as she sipped her tea.

"He's ugly." Traven said, looking at Cassie. "Are all the people of Sistra so ugly."

"No," Reuben said, "I believe he's an exception. I'll ask Micha to put a bag over his mug so it doesn't offend our lady."

"That's just mean." Barbara said, sitting up. "He is a handsome young man. You two rogues are hopeless."

Cassie laughed. "Jameson is a handsome man. Now let's knock off the insults. What do you know of him?"

Reuben did not smile. "Axel attacked Sistra first as we all know. They fought back boldly. King Hershell sent the Rangers to aid them. When we arrived Axel's army, who were an elite force, had pushed them back to the castle. The Rangers helped defeat them." He sat up, "Prince Jameson was still fighting as they were overwhelmed. The men followed him although he was very young. He is a fighter, and a leader; although he is ugly."

"You two boneheads are going to stop calling that young man ugly." Barbara said, staring hard at Reuben and Traven."

They both smiled.

"Shawn would know him." Traven said as he leaned forward. "Hickman and his forces were sent to Sistra. They supported their army. King James allowed Hickman to be in charge. The battles they fought were brutal."

Cassie stood up going to the door. "Micha would you have Shawn come in here."

A short time later Shawn stepped in, sitting down he was sweating and covered in dust. He looked at Reuben and Traven. You two enjoying tea with the Queen while I'm sweating with the army?"

"Enough Shawn." Barbara said, shaking her finger at him.

Casie tried not to laugh. "Prince Jameson from Sistra is visiting, and has requested an alliance. What do you know of him?"

Shawn sat quiet for a while. He sighed "I would follow that man to the gates of hell and kick it in if he was leading. He was young during the war and although a Prince, He fell in line and followed orders as did as any of us commoners." Shawn sat quiet for some time as the memories of the war flooded back. "His brother Amos was with Hollander, they were ambushed and we were told to reinforce them. We ran through the night and in the morning arrived at a small valley in the northwest. Jameson did not stop; he ran headlong into the battle and fought his way to his brother. He was cut up and bleeding, barely alive but did not stop fighting. He found his brother but he had died." Shawn stood up and walked to the door and stepped outside. The rest sat quiet.

Shawn stepped back inside after a few minutes. "I apologize to my lady. I had a piece of dust in my eye that was bothering me. Jameson is as solid of a man as ever there was one. I would trust him with my family." he looked down and said softly, "that includes all in this room."

Cassie cleared her throat and sipped her tea. "He is my guest. I believe you should have Micha take you to his room. I'm sure he would like to see the castle grounds as well as the army."

Shawn nodded and stepped out of the room.

Cassie spent the next several days speaking with Jameson. They agreed on an alliance and trade for the two countries. They talked of problems each nation faced. She would sit with him in the evening in the garden and talk with him. Cassie enjoyed spending time with Jameson. The subject of the war did not come up.

It was a cool evening as the fall nights were becoming cooler. Cassie smiled

"I am fortunate to have those closest to me as loyal friends." She looked at Jameson,

"I know they call me CC. Except for Reuben, he is always formal."

Jameson stared at the beautiful woman next to him on the stone bench. He removed his cloak and placed it around her shoulders. She smiled at him with her dark eyes that looked like deep pools of water. He leaned his head close to her then slowly leaned back not wanting to insult her. Cassie did not move as she looked into his green eyes.

Jameson looked off in the distance seeing the setting sun and the beautiful colors in the sky. He smiled as he turned to look at Cassie.

"My men called me PJ., except Shawn. I was named a captain over a unit he was at my side. I didn't mind." He was quiet for a while. "You know I had a cook once call me fancy pants."

Cassie giggled and put her hand to her mouth. "Really?"

"Yeah, I went to the Cook and told him the meat was too well done which made the meat tough. He said "Well fancy pants, you seem to have a sensitive palate. Perhaps you would like to come show me how to cook with the few resources I have and the thousands of men I am expected to feed." "I told him I didn't wear any different pants than others in the Army. The meals after that were better and the meat was not so tough."

Cassie laughed. "I don't suppose you told Shawn?"

"No, he's a little more sensitive than I am. You know my Mother when she gets irritated at me calls me James son."

Cassie laughed. "Do you irritate her often?"

"Yes, actually I do. She is quiet on the throne sitting next to my Father and in public, but when they are behind closed doors, she speaks her mind." Jameson looked into Cassie's dark eyes. "I believe you would like her."

Cassie stood up as did Jameson. She stood in front of him then placed her hand on his cheek and kissed him lightly on the lips. She smiled. "Good night James son. As she handed his cloak back to him."

Jameson left two days later.

Chapter XXV

Micha walked into Cassie's library holding a sealed envelope. He handed it to her, "Father Jacob brought this to you. He said it was urgent and is wanting to speak with you concerning the information."

Cassie reached out taking the letter. She looked at the seal seeing it was from the Pope. Her fingers trembled as she broke the seal and began reading. She smiled and handed the letter to Barbara.

"Tell the Priest he may leave. There is no reason to discuss the matter."

Barbara looked up from the letter smiling. "This is great news Cassie."

"I know. Cassie said, sitting back. "The Pope has stepped down because of health reasons, and Bishop Connors has been chosen as the new Pope." Cassie frowned "The coronation has been postponed for at least six months. I suppose the new Pope has a lot of duties. I am disappointed the coronation has been postponed." She sighed "I'll write an official announcement for the people. I'm sure the Priest is alerting the Nobles first." She looked at Beth who assisted Barbara. "Would you have Reuben step in please."

Beth immediately stood up leaving the room.

Cassie sat on her throne, she scanned the room seeing Reuben and his guards who were always on duty. Traven, Beth, Shawn, and Barbara as well as Micha. She smiled as she said, "Micha you have served me well and have learned under the direction of the Captain of the Guard." She stood up, taking a sword that was leaning against her chair. She walked toward Micha. "I have a gift for you," She handed him the sword. Micha looked at the sword surprised. "It was my brother, Michael's sword, your Father's. You will take his name which is appropriate. The records will reflect that you are Michael Conrad. I will still call you Micha. "

They were all surprised. Brabara immediately realized Cassie was recognizing his royal birth. Cassie smiled as she walked to Beth. She reached out holding both her hands. "I am told during the difficult days of Micha staying with that brute. You brought him food, blankets and clothing. I cannot express my gratitude for your kindness. You will be Lady Beth Tisdale from this day forward. You are the wife of the commander of my armies. You will be recognized for your work."

Tears ran down Beth's cheeks. "Thank you, my Queen." she said breathlessly.

Cassie hugged her. She stepped back. "I realize the difficult duty you have trying to keep Traven on the path of righteousness." She said smiling.

Beth giggled. "It is my burden, My Lady."

"I don't believe it's a burden to be married to the world's greatest lover." Traven said with a slight smile.

Cassie walked back to her throne sitting down. "Reuben, I need you to make arrangements to travel to Sistra. I want to see the people of my Realm as well as visit Sistra. Micha may assist you as he is promoted to the Queen's guard." She leaned over, staring at Reuben. "He is royalty, and you should remember that in his training."

Reuben in his stoic manner said "No, he is training as a Royal Ranger. Micha will be my second in command."

Cassie sat up. "Shawn and Barbara, along with Micha will travel with us. Traven you will be in charge of the castle until I return." Cassie leaned forward. "I expect you to make sound decisions. I do not want to return and have the dungeon filled with Nobles, or you giving them baths. I realize they can be difficult, but you have to show restraint."

Traven lookied serious. "As you command my lady."

Cassie sat back looking at Traven with a skeptical look.

Micha and Shawn sat on the bench seat of the Royal carriage two days later. Six powerful horses were hitched and anxious to move. Reuben on a horse was in front as six men of the Queens guard were positioned around the carriage. They all wore the blue and gold uniforms of the guard with the exception of Shawn who wore the blue and red uniform of the army.

Cassie hugged Beth saying "we will be gone probably three months. Please send me correspondence occasionally letting me know how it is going." She looked at Traven. "I have full confidence in you Commander. Please keep me informed of what is happening in the Kingdom."

"Hey Traven, don't be tossing anyone in the latrine, or dragging them behind your horse to fill in holes on the Queen's road." Shawn said, leaning back.

"You and me when you get back are having a talk of how to treat your betters." he said pointing at Shawn. "And don't be a bad influence on my friend Micha."

Shawn laughed. Traven opened the door and held Cassie's hand as she stepped inside with Barbara. "I will pray for you Traven." She said smiling.

The carriage left traveling through the busy cobblestone streets of Kachita. People removed their hats and bowed. The countryside was in bloom as it was early spring. A cool breeze with the sun shining made it a beautiful day.

The carriage would stop in small villages so Cassie could step out and speak to the people. They were excited to see the Queen. It had been many years since any of the villagers had seen or even spoken to royalty.

Their entourage stopped at the estate of Sydney Davis. It was obvious he was not pleased to see the Queen. His wife invited her in for tea. They were cordial to the Queen but also aloof. Sydney complained of how the surfs were often indigent and rude to him. Cassie nodded saying rudeness should not be tolerated. She also pointed out that since the change in the tax system where her men were now collecting taxes, even with the reduced taxes, There were more taxes collected. Sydney pushed the issue of Noble lords having more control of Surfs and their duties. Cassie put her cup down on the saucer looking at Mrs. Davis. "Thank you so much for your hospitality. You have been very gracious. She stood up walking out. She looked at Sydney as he followed her.

"You will do as the law commands or I will have Traven and his men pay you a visit. He will not be as patient as I am."

The carriage left the estate.

A small village of Norton was on the border of her Kingdom. The royal carriage stopped in front of a small Inn. The People were shocked as the Queen walked in with her Royal Guard. She approached a young girl who immediately went to her knees with her head bowed. Cassie reached out, helping her stand.

"I would like to stay in all your rooms."

The young girl looked up briefly then turned and ran to the back going through a large door. A woman in a plain dress wearing an apron walked out. She gasped and went to her knees. She had not believed her daughter who ran into the kitchen saying the Queen had arrived. She was shocked to see Queen Casandra

Cassie helped her stand. "I am need of all your rooms, would that be possible?"

"Yes, your Highness, all are available and have been cleaned."

They followed the lady upstairs where she showed each to a room. Later that evening the woman and young girl set the table with food and walked around the group seeing their needs were met.

The regular customers sat in awe sipping their rum seeing the Queen in their small village.

The following morning when breakfast was finished. Cassie walked up to the woman and said, "Thank you for your wonderful hospitality."

She handed the woman a small gold piece. The woman's eyes were wide.

"It's too much your Highness. I would be pleased to serve you with no charge." She whispered as a tear ran down her cheek.

Cassie kissed her on the cheek, turned and walked out. The Royal party would arrive in the capital of Sistra a week later.

Chapter XXVI

The King and Queen were standing on the large patio as the Royal carriage stopped in front. A royal guard opened the door and grasped the hand of Queen Casandra helping her out. He also assisted Beth.

Queen Esther hugged Cassie. "It is so good to have you here, Queen Cassandra."

"King James smiled, taking her hand. "Welcome Queen Cassandra."

"I am glad to see you are feeling better, King James. Jameson said you were ailing."

Cassie said, smiling looking at the elderly king.

"I have recovered with the help of my dear Queen." he said smiling. He turned to take Jameson's arm. "I suppose you remember my son Jameson. I hope he was cordial, my dear. Also my daughter Abigail, and her husband Franklin Dunst."

Cassie smiled at Jameson. "I do seem to recall a visitor from your realm Sire." She giggled as she looked at the smaller woman and man next to her. "It is a pleasure to meet you Princess Abigail and Prince Franklin." They both smiled and bowed to her.

King James stepped around Cassie looking directly at Reuben. He stood quietly staring at him. He cleared his throat and with emotion in his voice said low,

"You are a Ranger sir."

"Yes Reuben," answered.

"I would consider it a privilege if you would allow me to shake your hand." King James said, looking at Reuben.

Reuben stepped up to the smaller man extending his hand. "The honor is mine, King James."

King James reached out grasping Reubens forearm feeling the powerful hand grasp his forearm. "My eternal gratitude to you and all Rangers who arrived to beat back the evil scourge that attacked my realm unprovoked."

"It was a privilege to fight with your army." Reuben said, in his stoic manner as he looked down at King James.

King James held his grasp for a long time. He stepped back walking toward his guests.

King James escorted them to a room next to the throne room where food and drinks were sat out. They talked of how the kingdom of Sistra was rebuilding and were happy to have their wine now being sent to Seaside for transport. King James thanked Cassie for having her men in the Kings guard help escort the cargo.

Queen Esther smiled saying "would it be acceptable to have a word with you Queen Cassandra?"

Cassie said "Of course."

The men and women with Cassie were escorted out and to their rooms. Queen Ester leaned forward taking Cassie's hand.

"I believe in speaking plainly, my dear. We both have small kingdoms and I believe it would be a benefit for both realms to be combined." Cassie was confused as she looked at the older woman with white hair who was looking directly into her eyes. "Jameson is our only son. He is a good man and intelligent. I believe a marriage between you and he would combine our two Kingdoms making them stronger. Jameson is capable but with your assistance he would be a better ruler. You should rule as Co-Regents, not one over the other. I realize it is somewhat unconventional but it would be best. Then when you have children they would rule over one large kingdom. I want you to consider this as a possibility." She stood up "you should rest now, I realize you are tired from your trip."

Jameson stood silently shocked. His mother had caught him off guard. He walked to Cassie taking her hand helping her stand up. He walked out with her. Neither spoke as they walked up the stairs. He stopped at the end of a long hallway in front of a large door. He opened it and stepped back.

"I hope you were not offended by my Mother's bluntness. She can be outspoken and sometimes overbearing."

Cassie placed her hand on Jameson's face and looked into his eyes. She leaned forward and kissed him. "I was not offended. I find her proposal intriguing." She stepped into the room and shut the door.

Barbara helped Cassie remove her dress. Cassie laid down on a bed with a beautiful blue print bedspread wearing her undergarments. She lay quietly thinking of the proposal. She did like Jameson, and could see the benefit of having two Kingdoms combined.

After half an hour she sat up then stood up and put on her dress. She walked out of the room and knocked on the door opposite her. Barbara opened the door surprised to see Cassie.

"Could you help me button my dress?" She asked, smiling.

"Of course." Barbara stepped behind Cassie and buttoned the remaining buttons Cassie could not reach.

Cassie smiled slightly saying softly "Thank you," as she walked away.

Cassie was sitting on a stone bench looking out at the large garden and the rolling green hills. Jameson walked up "may I sit with you my lady."

"Yes of course."

Jameson sat down "I thought I would find you here."

Cassie turned and looked at Jameson. Neither spoke. Finally Cassie said

"Are you here to propose?"

Jameson was surprised by the question. He sat quietly then said "I'm afraid that you would be offended. I realize my Mother is pushing an issue that I am dragging my feet on. I have fallen in love with you and want to marry you more than anything in this world. I promise before the Lord if you marry me I will not ever try and rule over you. I love you more than my simple words can express and would trade my life for yours without hesitation. You are without a doubt the most beautiful, intelligent, intriguing woman the Lord has created. If you agree to marry me I will spend the rest of my life making sure you are happy. We will be co-regents. Will you marry me Casandra?"

"Yes."

Jameson smiled then laughed. "You have made me so happy." He leaned over and kissed her. He pulled her close as her arms went around his neck. She broke the embrace and looked into his eyes. "How long have you been working on that speech?"

"Since I first walked into your throne room."

"It was nice." She kissed him again.

Chapter XVII

Jameson was surprised as he walked out of the castle doors seeing Cassie standing next to a horse with Reuben, Shawn and Micha. She was wearing tight leather pants, a cotton shirt and a long cloak. He had expected her to ride in her carriage.

They had planned to travel throughout the kingdom to tour the countryside. He stepped down the stone steps walking up to her. He smiled seeing his horse was saddled.

"Did you oversleep? I was about to send Micha up to check on you." Cassie said, looking concerned. She bent her left leg as Reuben grasped it, lifting Cassie in the air onto her horse.

"I apologize my lady, I didn't realize there was a set time to depart." Jameson said, stepping into the stirrup and swinging into the saddle.

Cassie giggled as she headed for the gate. Reuben was behind her as were two of the Kingsguard along with her Queensguard behind him. Shawn and Micha brought up the rear.

Riding on the dusty road Jameson asked. "Since we are engaged, and by the way my Father plans on announcing the engagement next week at a large banquet in your honor. What would you like me to call you? CC?"

"You call me Cassie. I will call you Jamie in private."

Jameson shook his head, "I don't really like being called Jamie. Sounds like a little boy's name a grandmother would use."

Cassied smiled, speaking softly, "so when we are in our wedding bed, naked and in an intimate embrace and I whisper Jamie in your ear you won't like it."

Jameson looked at the beautiful woman in the tight pants and shirt that showed her figure. "You may call me Jamie or anything that pleases you Cassie." He took a deep breath and let it out slowly saying "You are just mean."

Cassie giggled.

The day was cool as the sun shined. The green rolling hills were beautiful. Cassie was amazed as she saw the grape vineyards with people in the fields. They stopped at an estate with a large two story house. There were large outbuildings behind the house. They were shown how the grapes were picked and prepared for making wine. Cassie was pleased to see the harvest of grapes. She was surprised to see young boys and girls with some women in large wooden barrels stepping on the grapes. The lord of the estate explained they were stomping on the grapes to extract the juice. It would be poured through a screen to have only juice and no skins, small leaves or stems. She said she had no idea that the grapes were stepped on for the juice. She smiled when Jameson said he and his brother and sister had spent time stomping grapes to help with the harvest. She did not believe him when he said he still had purple feet.

They would travel through the countryside seeing small farms and large vineyards as well as orchards. The Nobles were surprised to see Queen Casandra riding as opposed to using a carriage. They were polite but found it unusual. Many realized she had fought in the war and knew it was not uncommon for a Wixon woman to ride. They all had expected to see a Queen in a fine carriage wearing beautiful gowns.

The group stopped at an Inn while in the Northwest part of the Kingdom. The people living in the area struggled to make an income since the ground was not suitable for farming. Most of the people had small cattle operations or sheep herders with some goats. They were poorer than the other parts of the kingdom. Jameson had warned the group that there were also highwaymen who roamed the countryside and they should be prepared.

It was beginning to get dark in the twilight hours as the sun was setting. Micha gathered the reins of the horses as the others went into the inn. He walked down the dusty road toward the corrals where the livery stable was located outside of town. He saw a small house with a young girl who had stopped and was watching him. She was carrying a wooden bucket with fresh milk, wearing a plain yellow dress with a white apron. A white cloth was on top of her head holding down her red hair. She had freckles across her suntanned face. She was pretty. He smiled at her as he walked past.

He stopped suddenly as five rough looking men stepped out from the barn. Each of the men were wearing old dirty cotton pants and shirts. They wore large slouch flat brimmed hats. Their shaggy beards and long hair hung loosely down.

They approached Micha one saying "fine looking string of horses you have there lad."

Micha did not speak as he looked at the men with swords and daggers. A man stepped up grabbing the reins of the horses. Micha did not release the reins. He pulled his sword and sliced the man's hand. The outlaw released the reins, stepping back holding his hand as blood flowed. He began cursing as Micha pointed the sword at the other men.

The young girl who had watched Micha walk past sat the bucket down and ran to the Inn. She opened the door seeing men sitting at tables with tankards in front of them. Her eyes were wide as she said breathlessly, "there's a problem at the corrals with the handsome young lord with horses!"

Shawn was on his feet running for the door. Reuben and the Kingsgurard, Queensguard with Jameson and Cassie behind them.

Shawn could see as he approached the corrals Micha was backing up swinging his sword. Two men were down and two men were on horses racing away on the dusty road attempting to steal their horses.

Shawn pulled his sword stepping beside Micha stabbed the man in the throat. He fell. One man was on his knees holding his left arm near the shoulder as a man lay on the ground bleeding. A Queensguard ran out of the barn holding three horses. Shawn Reuben and a Queen's guard mounted. Reuben glanced at Micha seeing he was not hurt. "The Queen is your responsibility." He kicked the horse and followed Shawn.

Cassie looked at Micha. "You alright Micha?"

"Yes, the thugs tried to steal the horses. I'm sorry two got away with your horses."

"That's okay Micha as long as you're not injured." Jameson said as he had the two wounded outlaws picked up and carried to the Inn. The one killed he left. Cassie was shaken seeing Micha in a fight. She put her arm on his shoulder. And walked back to the Inn.

Shawn caught up to one of the men and a sword fight ensued as their horses were running at full speed. Shawn thrust his sword in the man's neck watching him fall. The Queensguard grabbed the reins of the stolen horses as Reuben closed in on the other man. He saw Reuben was close. He dropped the reins and raced forward. Shawn grabbed the horses and slowed down. The man died when Reuben caught up with him. The three men headed back to the small village with their horses in tow.

The horses were placed in the barn. Reuben stared down at the young man who was the owner. He said he did not know the men and they had threatened him.

Reuben glared at him. "Should any horse not be in the corral tomorrow? I will cut your head off and hang it in a garden to scare crows. I may do it anyway just because you lied to me."

The young man shaking stood closed mouth looking up at the huge man.

Cassie was glad to hear the horses had been recovered. Later that night Reuben told Micha he had done the Rangers proud. He had stood against five thugs.

Mica looked at Reuben. "I, well I didn't kill a man. I had an opening as you trained me, but I aimed high, stabbing the two men." Micha looked down.

Reuben put his hand on his shoulder. "You stopped the men. Sometimes it takes more discipline to not kill a man than to take a life. I'm proud of you. Justice will be given to the two who survived.

The following morning Micha was up early as was his normal routine. He had saddled the horses when he saw the young girl watching him. She smiled and said softly, "You were so brave my Lord."

Micha smiled shyly. "I was trying to protect the horses. Thank you for your help."

She walked up to him and pressed her lips against his. She stepped back smiling.

"I've never kissed a Lord before." She giggled saying "well I never kissed anyone before." Her cheeks were slightly red. Micha stepped up to her, putting his arms around her slim waist pulling her closer. Her arms were around his neck. He kissed her. Looking into her dark eyes said "I have never kissed anyone."

She smiled and kissed him again then stepped back and walked away.

Chapter XVIII

The two men of the Kingsguard rode ahead of the group at a casual lope. The Queensguard behind them. Jameson was anxious to return home. He knew his Father and Mother had planned a banquet in Cassie's honor and was planning on announcing their engagement.

Riding beside Shawn and Reuben Micha smiled as he rode.

Shawn said as they traveled, "you did well Micha, I'm proud of you and believe you are worthy to be a Ranger."

Micha smiling said, "I'm not tall enough to be a Ranger."

"I will make an exception to that rule. What's inside you is the courage and valor of a Ranger. You stood against five men, when others would have retreated." Reuben did not smile as he looked at Micha "It's a silly rule to have a Ranger be of a certain height."

Micha smiled knowing he was just under five foot five.

Reuben watched Micha then said "what else? There is something else going on with you."

Shawn laughed, "Let's hear it Micha, What is going on with you? Would it have something to do with the pretty milk maid?" He looked at Reuben. "She said the young handsome lord, as I recall.

Micha's face was red as he looked away. "She kissed me."

Reuben and Shawn smiled. "A fitting reward." Reuben said as he looked ahead.

They would arrive back at the castle two days later.

Cassie sat in her room which was dark with only one candle providing a dim glow. She prayed asking the Lord for strength and patience. She knew tonight would be a challenge. She needed to keep her emotions in check. Cassie had faced this same challenge many times in her life. Being from mixed races she often felt like an outsider, not accepted by either race. She was proud of her Wixon culture as well as her Caucasian race. Nobles were the same regardless of what culture they were from. She was royalty a Princess of both races, but many would not accept her because she was not pure blood.

Cassie stood up taking a deep breath when she heard the light knock on her door. She walked to the door, opening it. She smiled seeing Jameson. He reached out, taking her hand. Reuben was standing at the end of the hall.

A large crowd of people stood silently watching the young couple descend the staircase. They were both dressed elegantly. Smiling as they were greeted by finely dressed Nobles who had been invited to attend the banquet in Queen Cassandra's honor.

The tables were set with fine dishes. Only the finest food was prepared and set in elegant dishes on the table. The wine goblets were filled and people sat talking and enjoying their dinner. Musicians played a soft melody lifting the spirits of the people as they enjoyed their supper.

King James rose smiling. The crowd grew quiet as the elderly King smiled, lifting a golden goblet. "My friends, I welcome you tonight to this banquet in honor of our dear friend and ally Queen Cassandra." The crowd raised their goblets and sipped the fine wine. "I also am pleased to announce that my son Jameson will soon be crowned King as I have decided it is time for a younger King to take control of the realm."

The crowd sat quiet as they raised their goblets.

The elder King smiled as he scanned the crowd with his eyes, "I also am pleased to announce the engagement of Jameson and Queen Cassandra. Together our two kingdoms will be one. They will rule as Co-Regents ruling together."

The stunned crowd sat frozen in place. None of the Nobles had expected the announcement of an engagement. All eyes fell upon Cassie who sat next to Jameson. A murmur in the crowd began to go throughout those assembled. An older Noble man stood up lifting his goblet.

"A toast to King Jameson and his wife Queen Cassandra. May he rule these two Kingdoms wisely."

Casandra stood up smiling holding her goblet. She raised it then sat it down. She smiled as she looked over the crowd.

"I will rule as Co-Regent, and will not have a King or husband rule over me. I believe there has been some misunderstanding. King Jameson will be my husband, and I his wife. We together will rule as one over both Kingdoms."

When Cassie sat down the crowd was stunned.

"Ridiculous, " the man who had made the toast said, standing his face red with anger. "You will not rule when the King is appointed. You have declared war on all Nobles! Your lack of decency and respect will not be tolerated in Sistra!"

Cassie rose slowly and proudly looking at the man with contempt. She scanned the room, her dark eyes staring at each person. "Sistra would not be here today had it not been for the Royal Rangers sent from Wixon Island who came to your defense." She stepped away from the table as stared at the finely dressed men and women. "How many of you fought in the war. How many of you lost sons?" She looked at the Queen "Ask the Queen how it feels to lose a son. She knows. No, the Noblemen of this realm as in most realms chose to stay home as those who they considered less than them fought. I know you see me as a half breed mongrel and not of pure blood. I am a Princess of two races and I am Queen." She walked toward the tables of those who were nobles. "I find your arrogance insulting, and not christian. I have an Issue with an unchristian nation."

She walked out of the room as all sat quiet. Jameson stood up glaring at the crowd.

"There will be changes when I am crowned King. It is time to embrace the future, and with that will be a new era. Together both kingdoms will become stronger. Many of the old ways will no longer be accepted." He walked out to the room.

Jameson did not knock; he walked into Cassie's room. He saw her sitting in a chair with tears streaming down her cheeks. He walked to her pulling her up and holding her close hugged her tightly.

"You will marry me since you have already said yes. There will be no backing out. Together we will build a new future by ruling as one."

Queen Esther stood up slowly, her face red with anger. She stared hard at the crowd. She threw the napkin she held on her plate turned and walked away. King James walked to her, taking her hand and placing her arm through his arm. Together they left the room. Princess Abigail accepted the hand of her husband and walked out with him.

Several hours later King James walked into a small room sitting down seeing the Noblemen who were obviously upset. He did not speak as the men complained of how a King should rule and the Queen should support her husband. They were all concerned how the new Queen would treat Nobles since they had heard how she treated the Noblemen in her realm. None of them would allow the Queen to tell them how to run their estates. When they were finished King James stood up saying,

"You should speak to Jameson, he is the King."

The following day as the Noblemen of the realm ate breakfast with Jameson they explained how it was not tradition or right to allow a woman to rule. Jameson sat quietly and said nothing as he listened to the complaints which included she was not of pure blood, and her contempt for Nobles was not right.

Jameson sat back after the men had finished. He looked at the men and said,

"No." They sat quite not sure what to say. "Queen Casandra and I will rule together. There will be changes and if you do not want to accept them then you will be banished from this kingdom. Should you choose to rise up against me I will bring the army of Queen Cassandra to your estate and hang you. Should you or your wife's gossip about my wife who is your Queen, since she is of mixed blood, I will place you in the dungeon and confiscate your lands. Change is coming gentlemen. None of your advice is required or needed. I will consult my Queen on how this Kingdom will be run. You will follow the law as I and the Queen establish or you can leave."

Jameson stood up and walked out of the room.

Chapter XXIX

A messenger arrived from Kachita. Beth's letter informed Cassie a letter from the Pope had arrived. She did not open it and was sending it for her to read. She also said Johnathan Yearly, a nephew of Elias Waggoner had informed Traven he would be moving into the estate of Lord Hocking. Traven had words with the young man and told him he would wait on your approval before moving into the Dell estate.

Cassie handed the letter to Barbara as she opened the sealed envelope from the Pope. Barbara looked up, raising her eyebrow. "Traven had words? I believe Beth is being polite."

"I know," Cassie said, handing the Pope's letter to Jameson. "I don't want to think about what those words were."

She waited for Jameson to finish the letter. He looked up smiling.

"Jamie, would you ask your Valet to have Shawn, Reuben and Micha come in."

He frowned at her "why of course darling."

Barbara giggled, "I assume he doesn't like your nickname."

Cassie frowned as she saw Micha limping into the room. He was holding his right side. She looked at Reuben, not smiling. She took a deep breath. "We will leave for Kachita tomorrow morning. I have received information from the Pope that he will arrive in one month for my coronation. He will travel to Sistra the following month for Jameson's coronation. Then he will marry us the following month." She sat back as the group watched her. "I would like to be married in

Norton. It is a small village on the border of our two Kingdom. Nobles and common people will be invited. I know it is unconventional but I want all our people to witness the marriage. We will be married outside, not in a church." she looked at Jameson. "Will you agree, Jamie, I know your Mother will be disappointed."

"Actually I believe she will like it, Cassie."

Early the following day Cassie told the King and Queen goodbye. Jameson said he would go with Cassie since his Mother would be in charge of preparing for the coronation. He rode next to Reuben in front of the carriage. Shawn and Mica sat on top guiding the horses, the Queensguard followed the carriage. They arrived five days later.

Cassie sat quietly in her library. She looked at Traven, Beth, Shawn, Barbara, Reuben, Micha and Jameson. She took a deep breath. "All of you are my closest advisors and friends. I believe it would be best after Jameson and I are married, Shawn and Barbara travel to Sistra. Jameson has asked Shawn to be Commander of Armies. Barbara will be his Chief Clerk. Beth will be her replacement as my Chief Clerk."

She sat quietly. "Jameson has asked that Micha be assigned to the Kingsguard. He will train them as Royal Rangers, then when the Captain of the Guard retires, Micha will replace him."

Reuben nodded slightly.

"I agree," Traven said. "I have trained Shawn well and he should serve the King well." He looked at Jameson. "He should also help with the washing. He has good experience with that."

"You are a scoundrel Traven. I'm worried you won't have me to keep you out of trouble." He looked at Reuben. "Not a word big man."

"Enough both of you." Cassie said smiling. "So tell me what has happened in the kingdom since I have been away."

Traven said "not much. Everything was routine. A Nobleman Jonathan Yearly informed me he would be moving into the Hocking estate in an extremely arrogant manner. He also let me know, the crown would be replacing the furniture and livestock that had been stolen. I told him to wait until you returned and you would discuss it with him. We did have some words and he has chosen to speak with you my lady."

"The words you had with him to convince him to remain in Kachita until I returned. What were they?" Cassie asked, sitting back watching Traven.

"I politely informed the gentleman If he continued to defy you, I would pull his pants down, bend him over and pound sand up the crack of his backside."

Cassie closed her eyes as the others in the room tried not to laugh.

"I spoke with the gentleman and he did agree to wait for your return, your highness." Beth, who was nervous, said, whispering.

"Thank you Beth." Cassie sighed, as she looked at Micha. "Please inform Mr. Yearly I will speak to him tomorrow morning." She looked at Traven. "While you are outside with Shawn and the army."

Cassie immediately disliked Jonathan Yearly. He was tall, slender with a pasty white complexion. He looked soft, not having ever worked outside. He was dressed in fine clothes and had an arrogance about him.

He bowed saying "I've been waiting over two weeks for you."

"I am sorry for your inconvenience. I had matters of state to take care of." She said coolly.

Jonathan looked unimpressed, saying "Since the estate at Dell is currently unoccupied I will be moving in. I will require reimbursement for the items stolen including the livestock."

Cassie moved her head slightly looking at Reuben. "Please escort this arrogant rude individual from my throne room. Explain to him what manners are, and if I hear he is in the Dell estate you will pay him a visit."

Reuben moved quickly towards Jonathan who was surprised. Grabbing his arm in an iron grip he dragged the man out of the throneroom through the open door. Once outside Reuben threw the man down the stone steps. Johnathan immediately jumped up protesting as Reuben threw him into his waiting carriage. Reuben stepped inside, hitting him hard across the face.

"Next time you show disrespect to the Queen I will rip your guts out and strangle you with them." He hit the nobleman again grabbing his slack body pulling him so his face was close to his. "You go to Dell and I will ride there and drag your worthless body out of that estate and cut you into pieces for the crows to eat." Reuben stepped out of the carriage glaring at Jonathan slumped over the seat.

"Perhaps you should read the bible where it speaks of humility." He looked up at the stunned driver. "If you are still here before I count to five you will die a terrible death."

The driver left whipping the horses as they bolted out of the courtyard.

Reuben walked into the library seeing Jameson and Cassie speaking.

"Does Mr. Yearly understand the proper etiquette of meeting with myself?" Cassie asked, not smiling.

"He does." Reuben said in his stoic manner.

"Is he alive?"

"Yes?"

"Any broken bones?

"May have broken his nose when he stumbled down the steps."

Cassie sat back, "The steps? There seems to be a number of accidents on those steps. Should I have a mason look at them?"

"I'm not sure that is necessary. I'm going to the training ground to check on practice." Reuben said walking out the door."

Cassie smiled as she looked at a young man standing before her. His head was bowed, not looking at the Queen.

"You are Gavin Holt?" Cassie asked.

The young man looked up with his eyes whispering "yes your Highness."

Cassie sat looking at the young man who was handsome. He was slender and close to five foot nine with dark hair and dark eyes. His sleeve on his right arm was sewn closed as his arm was missing from the elbow down. He had been working with the groomsman since the war had ended. Gavin had fought for Axel during the war. He had lost his arm during a battle. Most men died when they received such an injury.

"You have sworn loyalty to me?" Cassie asked.

Gavin's head came up, his eyes met hers, "I have my Queen."

"My Valet has recently been promoted. I have received good reports of your work ethic and loyalty. I am promoting you to Valet. Beth will help you with clothing you will wear and Barbara will instruct you on your duties." Cassie leaned forward. "You will answer to no one but myself."

Gavin stood stunned as he looked at the beautiful Queen. He was a groomsman who was the illegitimate son of a Nobleman. He was not recognized since his mother had been a young girl who worked as a maid on his estate. He was told the Nobleman had taken her against her will.

Beth stood up from the table smiling, walking toward Gavin. "Let's you and I pay a visit to the tailor."

That evening Gavin stood up when he saw the big Ranger walking towards him.

Reuben stopped directly in front of the young man. He leaned over growling,

"Your life is not important, the Queen's life is. You will protect her no matter the situation or numbers. Do you understand!"

Gavin nodded "Yes, Sir."

Reuben handed him a large dagger. "Strap it on," he barked.

Gavin was able to quickly tie the large dagger on without any difficulty. He had learned to make adjustments using his left hand. Reuben handed him a wooden dagger used for practicing. He immediately swung the one he held as Gavin blocked it with the one he held. The dagger was knocked from his hand as Rueben slapped him hard across the face. Gavin staggered but did not fall.

"Pick it up." Reubeun growled.

Each evening Gavin would leave his duties as the Queens Valet, and report to the practice field.

The following weeks were busy as the castle prepared for the Pope, Kings and Queens who were invited along with their families. Nobles were expected. Martha Jinks, who was ten years older than Cassie ran the kitchen, informed Cassie what the meals would be and when she would serve them. Cassie looked at her and smiled. Martha was almost six foot with a muscular build and a pretty face. She had a large bosom and long red hair. She was the head cook and it was her kitchen no one crossed her. The meals were excellent and everyone who worked for her knew their job. Most of the girls and young women were orphans and widows from the war. It was said King Axel did not cross her. If anyone messed with one of her girls they would face the wrath of Martha.

Cassie smiled "thank you Martha If there is anything you or your helpers need please let me know."

Martha nodded and walked away.

Cassie sat in her library with Traven, Beth, Shawn, Barbara, Reuben and Jameson. All sat quiet as Martha explained the menu for the following weeks. She said "I don't care how the guests are arranged. My girls will serve all in attendance the same. If there is a special request for meat rare, well done or a special desert it will not be honored. I do not have time to serve sixty or seventy plates. My girls will not bring a plate back. If they are given a hard time I will deal with the issue."

"I doubt there will be any complaints since your food is always great, Jaxs." Barbara said, smiling."

"Thanks Babs, there always seems to be one who is a picky spoiled brat who wants to complain." Martha said, frowning.

"You have my support Martha." Cassie said smiling. "Which means the entire room."

Martha softened and smiled a rare smile "thank you Queen Cassandra. I want this occasion to go off without problems."

Martha turned to walk out. She hesitated as she glanced at Reuben. His eyes met hers for an instant before she walked out the door.

Cassie looked at Barbara. "Jaxs?"

Barbara laughed. "Martha and I grew up together. She was raised by Calvin Mooney. He was the head cook. Rumor has it she was the daughter of a Nobleman and a young girl who worked in the kitchen in the castle. Jaxs grew up working in the kitchen with her mother. Remember when your oldest brother Otis had a black eye and swollen nose. It was Jaxs who took him down for saying she had red hair because her brains rusted."

Cassie laughed. "Otis never told Father why he had a black eye."

Cassie sat quiet. Then sat up "Barbara, Beth I need you to have the tables set up and place name plates at each table. I would prefer the Nobles be at the back and not sitting with Royalty. We should have Royal families together and not mix them. Reuben can have Dalton and Gavin watch the tables so no one changes the name plates." She looked at Reuben. "Please indulge me, it really is important."

He frowned and nodded slightly.

Cassie took a deep breath. "I know there will be an extra amount of egos in the room with all those attending. Please everyone show restraint."

She looked at Traven, "everyone."

Cassie looked directly at Reuben, "Is there any possibility my Valet can attend this week without being bruised and bloodied?"

"No," Reuben said, "he is learning to fight with his left hand which is against his nature. He is a quick learner, but he has a long way to go."

"He doesn't have to be a Royal Ranger to be my Valet." Cassie said, leaning back.

"Yes he does." Reuben answered.

"No, I don't believe he does.

"I believe he does."

Traven leaned forward "I don't believe you will win this one my lady."

"I am the Queen."

"Royal Ranger, I believe that says enough. He will make sure you are protected by making sure only the best is with you. Although you can protect yourself." Traven said as he leaned back.

"I would let him have this one." Barbara said.

"Ok, so everyone knows I am the Queen. Gavin will be trained by Reuben as he decides."

"Good call," Jameson said smiling.

"Your training begins after you're married." Reuben said, looking directly at Jameson.

Jameson smiled as he stood up taking Cassie's hand as she stood up. The others all stood up except Reuben. They left as Reuben said in a quiet voice.

"I would like a word Cassie."

Cassie sat down as Jameson said "I will wait for you outside Cassie."

"You are welcome to stay, Prince Jameson." Ruben said, looking at him.

Jameson sat next to Cassie.

Reuben sat quietly for some time. He sighed "Rangers normally don't marry, because we are loyal to the crown. Some have but not many." He looked down which was the first time Cassie had seen Reuben look away. He looked up "I would ask your permission to marry Martha."

Cassie stood up going to Reuben, she took hold of his large hands in her small hands.

"You do not need my permission my friend. I give my approval and blessing." She leaned over, placed her small hand on his face, closed her eyes and began to chant. When she finished she kissed him on the cheek whispering "I love you Reuben."

Chapter XXX

The Royal families began arriving early. Rooms were made available for them in the Castle. Their Royal guards were placed in the army's barracks. The Queen's Army slept in tents on the practice field. The Pope was scheduled to arrive on Friday, and the Coronation would take place in the Church on Sunday.

Cassie met each royal family at the patio and graciously welcomed them to her realm. Some of the Kingdoms had fought with Axel however they pledged their loyalty and allegiance to her and negotiations for trade with her Kingdom began.

Cassie bowed low when King Jarrod and Queen Ola arrived. "I am so pleased you are here. You are most welcome."

King Jarrod kissed her on the cheek. "Thank you for the invitation. We are allies and friends."

"I have rooms prepared for you and your family. We will have tea in a short while."

King Jarrod turned, seeing a large royal coach arrive with men and women guards. He smiled seeing King Hershell and Queen Asha step out.

He grasped King Hershell's forearm firmly. "Hello my friend I waited for your arrival wanting to be the first to greet you."

King Hershall laughed as he looked at Queen Ola. "So happy to see you, Queen Ola. He kissed her on the cheek. You just arrived didn't you."

She smiled "Yes."

King Hershall kissed Cassie on the Cheek "I am so proud of you Niece. It is good to see you, Queen Cassandra Conrad."

"Thank you Uncle." She said bowing low. She reached out taking Queen Asha's hand "It is good to see you, Aunt Asha. Please come in and rest. We will have tea later."

In the afternoon the Royal families were called to the throne room for tea. The Nobles had arrived and mixed with the Royal families talking with them. Tables had been set up with names in front of each chair. The tables were set with cups and saucers and small plates. The royal guards for each family were stationed around the room. Each of them wearing dress uniforms with the family's Royal insignia.

King Hershell walked up to Reuben. "I was pleased to hear that a member of the Royal Rangers survived. You are Reuben Byne, Commander of the Rangers."

"I am."

"You defied my order when you were recalled. Your mission is to the Wixon Crown, you refused to obey my command."

Cassie had walked up to the two men. "Reuben is commander of my guard. He is serving the Wixon crown. My Mother, your sister, was a Princess of the Wixon crown. I am a Princess of the Crown. Reuben is serving the Wixon crown, Sire."

"I am the King. He will serve the King! You are playing on words, Queen Cassandra!"

The two stood silently staring at each other as the tension grew quickly. Tory Allan, who was in charge of the Queen's guard, walked up to Micha who was standing next to Reuben.

"You are a member of the Queen's guard." She said, smiling at him. Micah did not say anything as he looked up at the tall slender attractive women. "Do you know how to use that sword you wear, or is it ceremonial?"

Micha did not speak.

Tory's hand went to her sword and pulled it quickly bringing it down toward Mich. He pulled his sword, raising it quickly, blocking her sword. The two swords clashed violently as the two fought. Shawn and Traven with their men immediately pulled their swords. Reuben raised his hand, staring hard at them. They stepped back, replacing their weapons.

Tory stepped back, her sword pointing down. She stared at the smaller young man. She stepped forward lunging toward Micha. He blocked her shot as the two swords rang as the steel clashed. The swords were moving quickly as those in the room watched in awe. It was a fantastic display of swordsmanship.

Tory stepped back looking at Micha. She nodded approval at him and placed her sword in the scabbard. She walked to King Hershell saying. "I'm the best sword in the Guard. He has no doubt been trained by the Ranger. He is good. May I recommend Sire, we have four of our guards stay with the Ranger and train under him. They can then train our guard."

KIng Hershell looked at Reuben. "I believe that would be a good compromise. If it meets with the approval of Queen Cassandra."

"It does, I would be pleased to have your guard here Sire. However, I would like to correct one mistake." She stepped closer to Tory. "Second best sword in the Queen's guard. I still am the best sword in the Queen's guard. Once a Royal Guard always."

Tory drew her sword "You will have to prove that."

"Micha your sword." Cassie said, stepping toward him.

"Queen Cassandra!" Queen Asha said stepping forward "You my dear are a Queen and this is the throne room. Please conduct yourself as your station deserves Tory please step back."

Cassie stared at Tory who smiled replacing her sword and stepped back. She straightened up, turning to Queen Asha bowing to her

"You are correct, Queen Asha, I apologize for my lapse of judgment."

Martha stood in the back of the room with eight of her girls dressed in blue dresses with clean white aprons. They held platters of food and teapots.

"Royal Highness,and Nobles if you are through with the bold display of bravado, and swordsmanship, I am ready to serve tea." She did not smile as she stared hard at those gathered.

Cassie smiled, "Of course Martha. Ladies and Gentlemen, if you will take your seats tea will be served." She looked at Reuben, "Please take Micha, and all those of the royal guards out to the practice field or barracks." Reuben waved his hand as each guard walked toward the back door. As the guards passed her She raised her voice,

"I do not want any more demonstrations of who is the best. There will be no swordsmanship demonstrations, or boxing, wrestling or slings with rocks being hurled." The men and women nodded as they left.

Cassie walked to a table and watched as Dylan stood up pulling out her chair. She sat down as he pushed it forward.

"Thank you Dylan."

He grinned, "You're welcome Cassie.

The young girls walked around the room filling tea cups and sitting small tarts before each guest. A young woman sat a tart down in front of Russall Davis, a young nobleman. He reached over and rubbed her backside. She jumped back startled as he leered at her.

Martha immediately walked up to him saying, "you keep your hands off my girl."

He sneered at her arrogantly, "or what winch?"

Martha walked to Gavin removing his dagger. She walked back grabbing his shoulder pulling him back and leaning over placed the large dagger on his crotch.

"Touch one of these young ladies again and I will remove your manhood."

Sydney Davis was on his feet, his face red with rage. "How dare you threaten a Nobleman, you common winch!"

Gaven stepped close to Sydney.

"Perhaps you should teach your son proper manners." Cassie said calmly from her table.

"I will not have my son threatened by a whore. He is of Noble birth!"

Martha walked toward Sydney holding the dagger. Gavin placed his hand on her chest stopping her. "You should return my dagger, Jaxs."

"Her eyes were burning with rage. As her hand grasped the dagger tightly. Gaven carefully removed it from her hand, placing it in his sheath.

Cassie sat her cup down. "I believe it would be appropriate for you to apologize for your rude remark concerning my head cook who happens to be a good christian woman. Also your son should apologize for insulting the young lady." She picked up her cup, raising it to her lips, siping the hot tea.

Sydney laughed. "Apologize to a common guttersnipe!"

Cassie sat her cup down. "I realize you believe being of Noble birth your son has the right to rape a woman who is not of noble birth. All women are for his sexual pleasure. I have no doubt you have raped many common women yourself." She raised her cup to her lips and said "Gavin please have Traven step in here please."

Sydney's face was beat red. "Noble men have had certain privileges allowed them. I suppose your thug will arrive and beat every Nobleman and drag them to your dungeon."

Cassie held the cup sipping her tea, "that is what he normally does," Her eyes were locked on Sydney. "I suppose I could ask the Priest about what the Bible says about rape, but he would only make excuses for your son."

Queen Asha stood up "Gavan, please stop."

Gavin stopped at the door looking at the beautiful Queen. He looked at Cassie who raised her hand. He stopped and waited.

Queen Asha spoke in a calm voice. "Dylan please explain proper etiquette to the gentleman how he is to act while in the throne room when royalty is present." She sat down as Dylan stood up.

He walked to Sydney. "Sit down or I will remove you from the throne room." He pulled the chair out as Sydney hesitated then sat down with rage still in his eye. "Another outburst I will drag you out and take your life." Dylan said, speaking low. He walked around the table and placed his hand on Russell's shoulder squeezing it hard. "Touch another young lady, I will remove your hand with a sharp dagger." He walked to Martha, bowing to her. "I sincerely apologize for the rude behavior of the young man. It will not happen again." He smiled, taking her hand. "I want to compliment you on the best tarts I have ever had the pleasure to enjoy."

Martha looked into the dark eyes of Dylan. "Thank you my Lord." She whispered.

Sydney stood up. "We will take our leave"

Dylan walked up to him. "You have not been excused, sit down or you will lose your life."

Sydney sat down.

Dylan walked back, sitting down. "Thank you Dylan." Queen Asha said smiling.

She looked at Cassie. "Is your throne room always so chaotic?"

Cassie smiled "pretty much."

King Hershell laughed.

Chapter XXXI

Jameson knocked on Casie's door later that evening. He smiled when Barbara opened it. She stepped back as he walked into the room. He stared at Cassie who was wearing a beautiful light green gown. "I hope you like it. Green is the traditional color of Wixon Island." Cassie said as she turned for him to see the full gown.

"It is beautiful, and you are stunning." He said truly impressed."

"I will take my leave now, my lady." Barbara said, smiling as she bowed low.

Cassie laughed. "You should come with us."

Barbara held her hands up, stepping back, "No, Beth and I will have a quiet supper in my room. No sword play, or cutting off of men's pride and joy. Thank you, I will with respect decline the invitation."

Jameson placed Cassie's arm through his saying, "Shall we go my lady?"

"Yes my dear. Let's hope for a quiet meal."

"I have been praying for that." He said smiling.

They walked into the throne room seeing most of the guests had arrived. Cassie stopped and asked, "How is it going Gavn?"

"Fine my lady, I believe the Davis family have chosen to not have supper with you."

Cassie smiled slightly. "Good."

They walked around the room meeting and greeting people. Tables were sitting with plates and tall glasses. She smiled seeing Martha had done an exceptional job. She smiled at Jameson, "will you excuse me Jameson," as he spoke to several guests.

She walked to the back seeing several of the Royal Guards standing against the wall. She frowned as she stopped in front of Traven and Shawn. Traven had a swollen lip and his cheek was also swollen. Shawn had a black eye and swollen nose.

"I see my order was disobeyed as you show the battle scars of fighting. Was I not clear of any challenges or trying to see who is the better?"

"You were my lady." Shawn answered.

"We did win upholding your honor." Traven said smiling.

She turned to walk away. Looking over her shoulder said "I will reduce your punishment by half, but no more challenging other guards."

"Aye my lady" they answered in unison.

Super was served by the young ladies as Martha watched closely. There were no problems as each of the guests were gracious and said thank you as they were served. Jameson had brought wine from home and it was served with the meal.

King Jarrod sitting at Cassie's table said, "My compliments Queen Cassandra, the meal is extraordinary. I would ask your cook to come to my castle but frankly I am scared of her."

Cassie smiled, "Martha can be challenging at times."

"I am pleased with the progress of Dell. I did notice that the estate is vacant. I have a proposal I would like you to consider." King Jarrod said as he picked up his goblet.

Cassie sat her fork down and wiped her mouth. "I am intrigued, Sire."

King Jarrod smiled. "Ola has a nephew, Brandon Maroony. He is a good man who fought in the war, and served well. He is like his mother who is sensitive. Brandon has had a difficult time since the war has ended. I would like for you to consider allowing Brandon and his wife to move into the estate at Dell. He is very good working with cattle. I have had cattle bred with cattle from Wixon Island. I believe the cross of the two have made them much stronger."

Cassie's face was slightly red as she smiled. She realized King Jarrod was paying her a compliment. "I will consider your proposal Sire. I have to say I do like the idea of a man who has served being in the Dell estate."

Queen Ola said, "Brandon is sitting at the next table. Perhaps you could make time to speak to him."

"I will."

"Also, I did take the liberty to speak with your Captain of the guard and asked if he would allow some of my men to be trained by him. Hershell frowned but did say he had no problem with it. I would ask your permission."

"Of course." Cassie said as she picked up her goblet. "A toast my friend."

On Saturday the Bishop met with Cassie in her library.

He hugged her saying "I am sorry for the delay Cassandra." He sat down and continued. "The ceremony is quite simple. We will gather in the Church. I will place holy sanctified oil on my hands and pray over you as I place both hands on your head. I will then place the crown on your head and bless you and end in a prayer. It is actually a short ceremony. Now at the wedding, I plan on being more elaborate. I always did like a bit of flair."

Casie smiled taking the Pope's hand, "I have nothing against the former Pope but I am so pleased it is you doing the ceremony."

"I have to tell you Axel did protest your being named as Queen. The former Pope had him wait for months before seeing him. He told Axel you were recognized and would be blessed by his office. He told Axel to leave since he had never approved of him being King. His guards took him to the coast and placed him on a ship."

"I am glad to hear he is gone."

"I would ask a favor. It is only a request and is up to you. I am the last of my family and with my vow of celibacy there will be no one to carry my family name. Would you and Jameson consider allowing a child of yours to have the name Connors as perhaps a middle name."

"I would be honored if you would allow me to name a child after you." Cassie said, "Thank you." The Pope said as his smile grew.

The church was filled with people on Sunday morning as Casie walked down the aisle. She stopped at the end of the aisle and stepped on to the small platform and sat down on her throne. The Pope in his formal attire prayed, then poured oil on his hands and placed them on Cassies head as he prayed a blessing for her. Stepping behind the throne he reached over and placed Cassie's mothers crown on her head. He prayed and the ceremony ended. Cassie Conrad was Queen.

Chapter XXXII

Most of the Royal families left after a few days heading for Sistra. They would attend the Coronation of Jameson then head for the small village of Norton for the wedding. Jameson with Shawn and Micha headed for Sistra after a week. Martha hugged Micha telling him to come visit her. A single tear fell down her cheek as she watched him ride out. She had grown close to the young man. Reuben and Martha married and he moved in with her into the castle.

Cassie stood on the patio looking at the castle grounds. The royal carriage was waiting for her. She had the insignia of King Axel removed and her Father's royal insignia placed on the carriage. Reuben was in front with Traven beside him. The royal guards were behind the carriage. "We should return in two months." Cassie speaking to Gavin. "I don't expect any problems, please let me know if there are any issues."

"I will, your Highness. If there are any problems I'll talk with Jax." Gavin replied, looking shyly at Cassie.

She smiled, "that's wise."

Martha stood at the end of the patio. "I will see you in a few weeks at Norton."

Reuben nodded slightly to her.

Cassie stopped at the door as Evan held it. "I will see you in two weeks Martha."

"Safe travel your highness" She said smiling.

Cassie stepped inside seeing Barbara and Beth, the carriage pulled away. She looked out the window. "I miss Micha."

The royal carriage arrived two days before the coronation. Cassie stepped out seeing Jameson waiting for her. He walked down the steps hugging her.

"How was the trip?"

"It was good. I missed you."

He placed her arm in his and walked up the steps. She stopped seeing Micha standing beside an older man with gray hair as well as Shawn.

"You look good Micha. Have you been keeping Shawn out of trouble?"

"Yes my lady. It has been a chore." he said smiling.

"That is not true. No doubt the influence of Traven. I'll work on it, your Highness." Shawn said with a slight smile.

"I will talk to Micha."" Traven said, walking up behind Cassie.

"No, you will not. I will talk to him." Reuben said seriously. "You rif-rafs are a bad influence on Micha."

Cassie giggled as she walked in the castle.

That evening Cassie sat with Jameson, King James, and Queen Esther at a banquet. It was a pleasant meal as all the Royal families and Nobles of the realm had been invited. Jameson leaned over, speaking low, "not as exciting as your throne room."

When the dinner ended Cassie walked to her room alone.

The coronation of Jameson was much the same as hers. Cassie sat next to King James and Queen Esther. She could tell the Nobles were not pleased to see her. Jameson's sister told her the Nobles were complaining to Jameson about any changes that she would force him to make concerning their role in the realm. He had told them there would definitely be changes. He laughed saying he would not be forced.

Cassie stayed in the Castle for two weeks then headed for Norton. She was pleased to see so many tents that were surrounding the small town. A large number of people from both realms had come. She was told that a few of the Nobles had not arrived. She was pleased to see that Brandon and his wife Katie had arrived. He told her he had moved into the Dell estate and the cattle were doing great. Brandon said he had traveled throughout the area meeting all the Surfs. With more people arriving in Dell, houses were being built to accommodate them. He was excited which pleased Cassie.

Many people wanted to see Cassie and speak with her. She spoke to the common people who were polite. She also took time to speak to all Nobles and their families. She assured them she wanted to work with them. However, she was firm telling them she would expect them to follow her laws. Pope Connors had met with her and Jameson explaining the ceremony.

The day of the ceremony arrived and at noon Jameson and Cassie were married. It was attended by thousands. Many of the Noble families and some Royal families were not pleased that common peasants were allowed to attend the wedding of two Royal families. The celebration would go into the night.

Jameson and Cassandra walked to the Inn where they would spend their wedding night. The woman of the Inn was so excited she became light headed. She opened the door and watched as Jameson and Cassie stepped in.

Jameson closed the door and took Cassie into his arms pulling her close. He kissed her passionately. She held his embrace and whispered into his ear.

"Tonite I'm yours Jamie."

The celebration would last for two weeks. A large market was set up with everything imaginable to buy. Games were played as music was available throughout the day and dancing at night. Competition was available including strength, wrestling, boxing and archery. Many people were amazed at the accuracy Micha had with his sling. It was a time for Royalty, Noble families, and Surfs to mingle. Although there were some who disapproved, most enjoyed the celebration.

Jameson and Cassie would arrive back at the castle and stay for four months. They would travel to Sistra in the early winter. They had decided not to build one large castle but to maintain the two. It would give them the opportunity to travel throughout the country to see for themselves what was happening in their realm. They would rule as Co-Regents together sharing power.

the end

Don't miss out!

Visit the website below and you can sign up to receive emails whenever RB Parkline publishes a new book. There's no charge and no obligation.

https://books2read.com/r/B-A-PNYC-PDGEF

BOOKS2READ

Connecting independent readers to independent writers.